If Not for You

MARGARET WILLEY

If Not for You

For Theresa Thybault-Knecht, With my thanks + appreciation for a great Young Author's Day. Margaret Willey Feb. 1989

HARPER & ROW, PUBLISHERS
Cambridge, Philadelphia, San Francisco, St. Louis, London,
Singapore, Sydney
NEW YORK

To Rosemary Willey with thanks

If Not for You
Copyright © 1988 by Margaret M. Willey
All rights reserved. No part of this book may be
used or reproduced in any manner whatsoever without
written permission except in the case of brief quotations
embodied in critical articles and reviews. Printed in
the United States of America. For information address
Harper & Row Junior Books, 10 East 53rd Street,
New York, N.Y. 10022. Published simultaneously in
Canada by Fitzhenry & Whiteside Limited, Toronto.
Typography by Joyce Hopkins
1   2   3   4   5   6   7   8   9   10
First Edition

Library of Congress Cataloging-in-Publication Data
Willey, Margaret.
  If not for you.

  Summary: A fifteen-year-old, trying to learn the
meaning of passion, is intrigued by the lives of a
married teenage couple and their baby.
  [1. Marriage—Fiction   2. Interpersonal relations—
Fiction]   I. Title.
PZ7.W65548If 1988   [Fic]   88-3343
ISBN 0-06-026494-2
ISBN 0-06-026499-3 (lib. bdg.)

What pulls at you when you come here,
pulls you away from what you know?
Will you be sorry if you stay?
Will you be sorrier if you go?

Dear Lou,

Writing you tonight from a little motel just outside Columbus. It's 11:00, and across the room on a saggy old bed is Raymond Lee Pastrovitch! I wish I could put into words what it does to me inside to see him asleep with his big arms curled up underneath him like a little kid and his curly hair all wild on the pillow.

Are you wondering yet what we're doing in Ohio? Because when I tell you, you will be the only person on earth who knows where we are.

We did it, Lou. Me and Ray. Like a couple of bandits. We got out of St. Martins! Did you think you were the only one who could get away?

Believe me, my way was a lot crazier than yours.

1

None of this moving-away-with-my-parents stuff for me. We cut out after Homecoming in Ray's new car— a rebuilt Audi from his uncle—bright red! I wore this incredible strapless dress, the same color. And Ray had a red silk shirt under his tux, and his hair is real long now. You would have dug it so much, Lou. We drove practically all night singing to the radio and laughing our heads off. God what a night! It was worth anything that happens now.

We're going to keep heading south in the morning. Ray has some friends in Florida. We might hang out there for a while, live on the beach. Ray wants to buy a tent. I don't really care where we go. I'm having so much fun—I feel like I'd go to Cuba if Ray said let's do it.

And you were wrong about Ray, Lou. Remember how we used to say we never could find the One? Lou, he's the One. I can't even tell you what it does to me when he puts his arms around me and gives me that look. Sometimes I feel like somebody unscrewed my head and poured in too much love and I can't keep it all inside. I just want to glue myself to his chest forever. And the thing that just tears me up is that he feels the same way. It's too much. It's beyond everything I used to want. Oh god, I'm so happy.

Don't you tell anyone what I said about Florida. If they ask you if you've heard from us, just say we're *fine, but you don't know where we are. I'll tell them soon enough. Right now, we feel so free. I haven't felt so free since the old days with you. Old friend, do you think I've totally lost it? I have!*

More soon. In love,
Linda

ONE

SMHS COUPLE DISAPPEARS AFTER
HOMECOMING; POLICE SEEK
CLUES TO WHEREABOUTS

ST. MARTINS, Oct. 15—Police are
investigating the disappearance of
popular St. Martins High School senior Linda Mason and her date at the
Homecoming Dance, Raymond Pastrovitch, after a good-bye note ad-
dressed to both students' parents was
found in Linda Mason's car. They were
last seen in the SMHS gymnasium,
where the annual dance was held Friday night. On behalf of the two fam-
ilies, and with the cooperation of

4

SMHS Principal Bernard Weber, police are seeking the whereabouts of the two students, to be sure that no foul play is involved in the incident.

She did it, I thought. *She got away from St. Martins.* And only a week ago I had seen her new dress, laid out on the sofa in her living room. Jenny had shown it to me—a gorgeous red strapless with a ruffled skirt—a dress a person would wear to accept an Oscar in. God, what style. I could picture their getaway. It gave me chills to imagine them running from that pathetic old building, lit up with ugly, faded lanterns, full of other seniors pretending to be doing something exciting. I pictured them speeding through the downtown and farther, along the lake to the expressway and away. It was October, but I was sure they'd had the top down, with their hair blowing, laughing.

I had a million questions to ask Linda's sister, Jenny. I couldn't wait to call her.

"I can't believe they actually *did* it," I cried when she answered the phone.

"You *know*," Jenny exclaimed softly. "How did you know, Bonnie?"

"I read it in the paper. When I got home from school."

"In the *paper*!" Jenny wailed. "It's in the paper?"

5

Before I could ask her anything else, she hung up. When I told my mother that Jenny had hung up on me, she shook her head.

"You mustn't bother the Masons," she said quietly. "They're probably all terribly upset. Evelyn must be so worried."

"Mom, Linda's with Ray," I reminded her. "It's not like she's been kidnapped. They just did it for fun—for fun—for a thrill. That's the way they *are*."

My mother was frowning at the article in the paper. Linda's senior picture was under the headline—she looked on top of the world, completely victorious.

"How could she do something like this to her mother?" mine wondered.

"Oh, Mom," I sighed. "She didn't do it *to* her mother. She did it *with* Ray."

I remembered seeing her on the beach in St. Martins the summer before, walking along the water's edge. I was sitting on a towel beside my mother, who had packed a picnic for us. Linda was wearing a black bikini. She looked curvy and tanned, and she walked with her head high, like someone who is perfectly happy with who she is and what she looks like. Her dark hair was pulled up into a curly ponytail that showed off her chiseled face and her wide smile. There were three boys with her, trying to be the one who said something that made her laugh. Linda recognized me as her sister's new friend. She waved, her smile bright, easy. And all three boys turned quickly to see who had distracted her, then quickly looked away from me in my shapeless Speedo. But Linda's smile had lingered.

"Who was that, honey?" my mother had asked.

"Jenny's sister," I said. "Isn't she beautiful?"

"Very pretty," my mother agreed. She was herself very pregnant with my brother Ben, and we both watched wistfully as Linda's perfect shape grew smaller, the three boys orbiting around her.

Soon after that, Jenny told me her sister was finally going steady.

"I'm not impressed with the guy," Jenny said. "He's kind of wild, and I don't think he's very smart. But it's a relief not to have all those other guys calling all the time."

I wondered which of the three was the winner. Soon I would learn that it was Ray Pastrovitch and that he would never have scampered alongside any girl, anywhere. Ray was the type to have his own followers, with his head of blond curls and his broad shoulders. They became king and queen of the beach that summer—the summer I decided I would give up the sun until I looked better in a bathing suit and wasn't so shapeless.

Linda and Ray were together in the fall—seniors where Jenny and I were starting out as freshmen. The sight of Linda and Ray arm in arm in the halls comforted me—I felt connected to their glamor because of Jenny, although they hardly knew me. But Jenny seemed to dread the sight of them.

"They're too *showy*," she said. "Like they expect everybody to bow or something. And they're always hanging all over each other."

"They stand out because they're so cool, Jenny," I insisted. "You're *lucky*."

Jenny scowled. "Sure, that's what everybody says."

I was convinced that the advantages of being Linda's sister outweighed the disadvantages. To actually live under the same roof with someone who had completely mastered high school! So what if sometimes you felt a little jealous? Besides, how could it be worse than being a teenager in a family that was totally mesmerized by a *baby*?

I watched Linda closely, hoping to learn what she'd learned before she left town for college or an exciting career somewhere. I watched her from the windowless halls of St. Martins, peeking out from behind my locker door for a passing glimpse. Linda and Ray were still tanned from summer. Their faces were always glowing, and they clung to each other as they walked. It seemed to me that they were too much for that school and that town— too happy, too wonderful. Too alive. They *had* to break free.

TWO

After I had asked Jenny for the third time if she thought Linda and Ray were going to get married, she put her hands over her ears.

"Don't even mention her name to me, Bonnie! As far as I'm concerned, I don't even have a sister anymore."

There were more and more rumors. The entire high school was caught up in what Linda and Ray had done, and people assumed that Jenny was in touch with them, although I knew this was far from true. Nobody had been as unprepared as Jenny for all the scandal.

"If she did call me, I wouldn't talk to her—I'd hang up on her!" Jenny cried.

I tried to imagine where Linda and Ray might have gone—a big city? a secluded resort? a romantic hotel? I sifted through the rumors, trying to unravel them. In the halls I would drift to the edges of conversations about the runaways.

"I'm not surprised Linda did it," someone said from a group of seniors outside her homeroom. "But what was Pastrovitch trying to prove? He can't be planning to settle down!"

"Who says they're settling down?"

"Linda did have quite a bit of money."

"Ray's not after money. He'd be happy for the rest of his life with an old car and a surfboard. She must have done something to him."

"I bet she's pregnant."

"Has Lou heard from her? Has anybody tried calling Lou?"

"Lou thinks it's just a joke that went too far. Because they were bored."

"I don't believe it was just a joke. Hey, those two are really in love."

"Yeah, and they wanted to get out. Nobody's gonna tell those two how to live."

Jenny started hating St. Martins for its small-town nosiness. "I feel like I'm living in a tacky country-western song," she said, "and it'll get even worse when she comes back."

"They're coming *back*?" I asked breathlessly.

Jenny frowned. She lowered her voice. "We got

11

a letter. She'll be back at the end of the month."

"You're kidding! With Ray?"

"Of course with Ray."

"Oh." I was silent, savoring this confusing news. I was both glad and shocked. What point was there for them in coming back?

"She's pregnant," Jenny added. She said this coldly, challenging me.

"I figured *that*," I lied.

Jenny put her books down slowly and covered her face. Her voice was muffled. "Throwing it all away," I heard.

"Oh, come on, Jenny," I protested. "This happens to lots of girls. It's not as big a deal as it used to be."

Jenny lifted her head. "Lots of girls do not stage everything like a Broadway musical comedy. And my parents are *completely* wrecked."

Suddenly I was defending Linda. "They should be proud of her," I insisted. "And so should you!"

Jenny looked appalled.

"Yes, proud of her," I repeated. "She's living her own life. She's not letting anyone tell her how to live. Everyone admires her. You should hear all the positive things people say about her."

"She dropped out of high school!" Jenny cried. "She's eighteen! She's pregnant! I can't believe what you're saying!"

12

"I can't believe what *you're* saying," I retorted, "about your own sister."

When I got home that day, I found my mother sitting on the sofa reading. Ben was asleep in her lap.

"Jenny Mason is so narrow-minded!" I said.

My mother looked up from her book, her expression worried. "Now what do you mean by that, honey?" she asked.

"She's terribly old-fashioned. I didn't realize it until this stuff started with Linda."

"I'm sure this has all been very hard for Jenny," my mother said. "She's a very private, sensitive girl. And a *good* friend."

"She's changed, Mom," I insisted. "I should know."

But she shook her head. "Didn't we just talk about this sort of thing before, Bonnie? Don't you remember?"

She was referring to a talk we'd had months ago. My mother was afraid that I was too critical of my friends. "No one can ever be exactly who you want them to be," she'd said, and I'd defended myself by saying that it wasn't my fault that Sandy, my best friend before Jenny, had been such a disappointment.

"Mom, this is different," I insisted. "This thing

about Linda has really affected Jenny. She hates school, she hates all her classes. She's *too* negative now."

"Of course she is, Bonnie. Don't you see that it's understandable that she would resent all the curiosity about Linda?"

When I sighed with exasperation, she leaned forward as much as she could without waking Ben. "Bonnie, you can't just dump your friends whenever they have a problem. You'll always end up alone. You'll never really get close to anyone."

I was glad Ben was holding her to the sofa. He jerked every time she even slightly raised her voice.

"I *do* know that, Mom," I said patiently, backing out of the room.

There was too much she didn't know. She didn't realize how much I admired Linda. She didn't realize how ordinary my life was beginning to feel. I needed a friend who *did* understand. A friend who dared to be different.

Dear Lou,

Your letter really hurt me. Is that what you wanted? Did you want to make me cry? Don't you know I feel guilty enough about not telling you I was pregnant? I bet I have a dozen letters to you that I started but never mailed. Because when I tried to put into words all the changes—the baby and getting married and everything—I just didn't know where to begin! Then I would end up feeling really far away from you and from the old days and all the things we did. And that would be too depressing, and so I just never found a way to tell you. I'm happy with my new life, even though everything is completely different now. Sometimes I can hardly believe it's still me. Some days I still feel a little weak from having the baby (did Mom tell you that I had a C section?). And then to get a

15

letter like yours, well, that's enough to screw me up for days.

I don't blame you for being mad because I didn't write. But you sounded all freaked out because Ray and me are back in St. Martins. All that stuff about me going backward instead of forward. Lou, I think you're about as wrong as you can be. You've always been kind of critical of Ray and that whole south-shore crowd, but I just have to say this—and I'll say it a million times if I have to—you just don't know the Ray I know. How could you know him? How could you even think you know him? You only saw one side of him. The drop-dead cute side. Remember how you used to tease me and call him Stingray? Remember how I called you the morning after my first night with him? But Lou, that was a different Ray than the Ray I married. And that was a different Linda, too.

I love him so much. He just makes me melt every time I look at him. I'm crazy in love with him. I'd do anything for him. I just want to make him happy. And now that we're married and we have Jeremy and we're an actual family, I don't feel the same way I used to about St. Martins. I don't mind being here— it has a whole new meaning for me, because it's the place where Ray and I first fell in love, first kissed, first made love on the beach. And we have that same beach just a few blocks away. And we have our own *place and our own life and we have Jeremy. It's home to me now, it really is.*

Lou, I'm sorry you had to hear about my baby from Mom. Please, please don't be mad that I didn't tell you myself. When you meet Jeremy, you'll forgive me.

Please don't write a letter like that to me again. Sometimes I can't believe you're that far away. Remember how we used to dance our brains out at Jake's until closing? Remember how we used to roar down to the beach in your VW? Remember the first time we saw Ray and he was wearing those ripped jeans and we watched him for half an hour, just waiting for him to turn around? We had a blast, didn't we? Please, Lou, don't be mean. From now on I'll write more, I promise.

Love you,
Linda

THREE

Jenny was wrong about a second wave of scandal when Linda and Ray came back to St. Martins. Runaways were big news at our high school, but dropouts and teenage pregnancies weren't. We had those every year. Linda and Ray got quietly married and settled into an apartment. Soon after, Linda had her baby.

"What a shame," my mother said when I told her. "Gee, that really makes me feel sad."

"She's extremely *happy*," I insisted. "Jenny told me."

Jenny hadn't, but this seemed to cheer my mother. "Is she?" she asked. "Well, why not, maybe she is."

Jenny still refused to even discuss Linda. We didn't talk about much of anything anymore. Jenny

18

had some new friends; they were private-school kids, and they didn't know anything about Linda.

I was surprised when she asked me to a family barbecue in May. *Why me?* I wanted to ask. Why *now?* I figured it must be because she didn't want to explain Linda and Ray to any of her new friends.

"Will Linda be there?" I asked, trying to sound nonchalant.

"They'll *all* be there," Jenny said darkly. "But you have to promise not to mention them running away. My parents are pretending it never happened."

"Where is Linda?" I asked Jenny as soon as I arrived for the barbecue at her house.

"On the patio." She led me to the sliding glass doors and pointed. Linda was sprawled in a lawn chair with her arms crossed on top of her head. Her face was pale and puffy, and she had dark circles under her eyes. A wave of surprise and concern washed over me.

"She's wrecked from having the baby," Jenny announced. She sounded triumphant, as if she had intended to prove something to me. "Can you believe it's her?"

I didn't answer. We went back through the house together and into the front yard. Jenny pointed toward the garage. A red car was parked there, with a pair of long muscular legs showing from beneath one bumper.

"There he is," Jenny whispered. "Where he belongs."

I had never heard her sound that bitter. It made me want to go home. Before I left, I stood a moment in front of Jeremy's baby carrier, looking down at him—Linda's baby. He was a funny-looking baby: He had a round, bald head and wrinkles under his eyes like an old man. I couldn't help smiling at him. He smiled back.

During the last week of school, Jenny and I were walking home in silence, all too aware of our crumbling friendship, when ahead of us I recognized the small, dark-haired figure of Linda, pushing a stroller toward us.

"Oh, great," Jenny whispered. "Turn this way before she sees us."

"She's already *seen* us," I said. "She's looking right at us."

Linda came toward us with her chin lifted, half smiling, still pale, but with her eyes bright. Her expression was ironic; I think she knew what Jenny thought of her, but didn't care. That day she looked young and thin in a jean jacket and a tight skirt, with running shoes on her feet. I was surprised at how young she looked—younger than Jenny, who, like me, made a special effort to look older.

"Hi, Linda," Jenny said flatly.

"Hi yourself. What are you two doing downtown? Is school out already?"

"We just got out," I said. "It's around three thirty." I leaned over and looked at Jeremy. He was asleep with a grin on his face. He looked so funny, smiling up at nothing, that I couldn't help giggling, and Linda laughed with me.

"Isn't he a rip?" she said. "Whenever he feels the sun, he smiles like that, awake or asleep. He's going to be a beach bum like his daddy."

Behind me Jenny snorted rudely, but Linda didn't react. "I'd better get him home," she said. "He'll wake up hungry."

She looked up at me. Her eyes were bright green. "What was your name again?" she asked. "Bonnie?"

I was flattered that she remembered. I nodded. She walked away from us with a backward glance, something wistful in it.

"She sure looks a lot better than she did at your house," I said pointedly. "Are we close to where she lives?"

"They got an apartment on Baker Street," Jenny grumbled. "It's really a dive. Ray doesn't have any money at all."

"He's just getting started," I said. "Lots of couples don't have any money when they get started."

Jenny gave me a piercing look. "Lots of couples aren't stupid enough to get married without finishing high school."

"You are such an incredible bitch," I yelled. "You can't even give the time of day to your own nephew. And you didn't even say good-bye to Linda. What's the matter with you?"

Jenny looked stunned, then scornful. "*You* try having a sister who everybody says is God's gift and then who embarrasses you to death at your own high school. You try it and see how you like it."

"I'm so tired of hearing about how embarrassed you are. You should be proud of how—"

"Oh, please, spare me that you-should-be-proud crap, Bonnie. It makes me sick."

She stormed off down the block. I didn't care. Jenny and I were too different. My biggest concern was that it was the end of the school year—summer was days away. I would be alone, as my mother had warned, without a best friend for the summer.

Dear Lou,

I've been wondering and wondering why you haven't written me back. I was afraid you might still be mad at me. Then I realized that the last time I wrote you, I never sent you my new address! What a dummy! We're right near the downtown on Baker Street—remember that all-night doughnut shop we used to go to after parties? (Except now it's a little grocery store where I buy baby food for Jeremy.) We have an upstairs apartment. It's so wonderful to have our own place! We paid for everything ourselves (I still have a little college money left). We didn't ask my parents for one lousy dime! I never ask them for anything. They would just use it against Ray. He has a job now, working for his uncle at the foreign-car garage, but they don't give him any credit for it—you know how

23

materialistic they are. They still have a real negative attitude. And my sister is as big a pain as ever. I could really use a baby-sitter these days—Ray wants to start going to parties again—but I'd die before I'd ask Jenny. Sometimes I wish you were here and you could help me with my baby. You always were so great with kids. God, I miss you so much!

We're doing fine. Baker Street isn't exactly north shore, but it's home. I'm going to get a job, too, when Jeremy's a little older, and then we'll be able to find a bigger place with a yard.

Anyways, old friend, now you have my address, so you have no excuse not to write back soon.

Love,
Linda

FOUR

I spent the entire first week of the summer alone in my room. When I got a call on a Saturday afternoon, I was thrilled that someone had remembered I existed.

"Is this Bonnie?" a voice asked. "Jenny's friend Bonnie? This is Linda Pastrovitch, Jenny's sister. Do you remember me?"

"Oh, *yes*," I said in amazement. "I remember you."

"Well, I have a little problem. Ray and I want to go to a party tonight, and I seem to remember that you have a baby brother and—"

"Do you want me to baby-sit?" I exclaimed.

"If you're not busy," Linda said. "Jenny's always busy on Saturday nights, so I thought maybe—"

"I'd love to baby-sit! What time?"

"Could you come around 6:30?"

"Oh, sure! You don't have to pick me up either. I live really close to Baker Street, and I have a new bike I can ride. Just give me your address."

"Are you sure?" Linda sounded like she couldn't believe her good luck. "That's fantastic. I'm so relieved. I didn't know you lived that close. God, I'm glad I called you. Fantastic!"

When I hung up, I felt like screaming. Baby-sitting for Linda and Ray! And she had sounded thrilled to have me. I couldn't believe it.

"Was that Jenny?" my mother asked from the kitchen table. "I haven't seen Jenny in weeks."

"Jenny's out of town," I said quickly. "That was her sister, Linda. She wants me to baby-sit."

"Linda? The one who . . . ? Really?" She sat thinking a moment before she lifted another spoonful of applesauce into Ben's mouth. "Help her out any way you can, Bonnie," she said quietly. "Do her dishes. Pick up her house. Throw in a load of laundry. And don't charge her extra for it."

"Oh, Mom," I said. I resented her misplaced sympathy for a Linda she didn't know.

"And invite Jenny over," she added before I

26

could leave the room. "The minute she gets back. I miss her."

Their apartment was the second floor of a bleached, porchless house that looked too small to even have an upstairs. The steps were in the back, and I climbed the rickety planks slowly. When I was halfway up, Linda opened the back door above me and stepped out onto a small landing. She smiled down, her hair fluffed out around her face, her eyes shining under thick bangs. It was the Linda I remembered from school. She pointed at me and laughed, her eyes crinkling. I looked down at myself and saw that we were wearing identical fuchsia sweatshirts.

"Love your sweats," she congratulated me. "Come on up. And you're on time, too! Jenny would have been at least an hour late."

I followed her into a narrow kitchen with a table, two chairs, and a high chair at one end.

"We're a little behind schedule ourselves," she said. "Ray!" she called behind me. "Jenny's friend is here!" She lowered her voice and put her head close to mine. "He's been in the bathroom for hours," she said, rolling her eyes. "Primping for the party."

I nodded.

"Here, let me show you around. It will take about five seconds—it's the tiniest apartment in the world."

It was so small that we had trouble walking through the rooms together. The ceilings were low and the floors all tipped to one side—I felt like I was walking through a miniature houseboat. There was only one small bedroom, and Jeremy slept in a crib against the wall opposite Linda and Ray's double bed.

"This is Jeremy's suite," Linda whispered. Jeremy was lying on his back with his hands over his bald head, his fists curled shut.

"He has pretty strange sleeping habits," Linda said, smiling down at him. "He'll wake up in an hour or so, and then I'm afraid he'll be up until around eleven. Or even later. If you can get him back to sleep before we come home—"

She stopped in mid sentence and shrugged, like this was too much to hope for.

While she was giving me instructions for Jeremy's supper, Ray came out of the bathroom in a cloud of steam. He was wearing a Hawaiian shirt and baggy white shorts, and his bare feet squeaked on the floor. He already had a dark tan. He looked at me curiously. The whole apartment seemed even smaller.

"Jenny's friend, right?" he asked. He took a step

closer and loomed over me, holding out his gigantic hand for me to shake. He smelled overwhelmingly of lime.

I shook his hand. "Are you leaving me a phone number?" I asked dazedly.

"It's right there," Linda said, pointing to the telephone. "But I should warn you—we're going to a pretty wild party. God knows who might answer the phone." She giggled at Ray.

"Let's hope it isn't Les," Ray joked back. They both laughed at this thought while I stood smiling awkwardly. Linda noticed and patted my arm.

"Don't mind us. This is our first party in a long time. Since Jeremy was born."

"But it sure won't be our last," Ray added. "Summer is *here*." He put his brown arm around Linda's narrow shoulders. She smiled up at him and half closed her eyes.

"Let's go," he said softly, hugging her.

"A few more things, Ray," she said, turning back to me. "We don't have a TV yet," Linda said apologetically. "We're saving up for one."

"I don't mind. I brought something to read," I said. I never went anywhere without a detective novel.

Linda put her head close to mine so Ray wouldn't hear, and asked softly, "And will you call me if Jeremy cries too hard?"

"I will," I said. "Don't worry."

From the living-room window, standing to one side of the faded curtain, I watched them leave. They walked to Ray's car in the driveway and smiled at each other over the black top like they were about to do something incredibly romantic. They had probably looked at each other the same way just before they roared out of St. Martins after Homecoming. They were such a *couple*. And only a few years older than I was. The Audi pulled away and screeched at the corner.

I wandered back to the kitchen. The refrigerator was stacked with Ray's beer, the narrow counter lined with spices, cannisters of tea and coffee, a stack of women's magazines. The bathroom was still warm from Ray's shower, with his razor and after-shave on the sink, his deodorant and two toothbrushes on the wall. Both their bathrobes hung from the bathroom door—Ray's huge and striped, Linda's white. Stacked behind the tub were toiletries and health aids—generic aspirin, diapers from K-mart, Ivory soap—all bargains.

I went back to the living room. There was a framed picture of Linda on the end table beside the sagging sofa—her senior picture, the one they'd used in the paper. Her smile was dazzling. She looked like a person who had leaped into adult-hood on a dare, leaving behind her childish high-school world. Now she had another world, a miniature, packed-to-the-walls world, full of responsibility. I wondered if I would ever in my life look the way Linda looked inside that cardboard frame—that eager for adulthood, that sure.

A sharp cry came from the bedroom.

Jeremy's cries turned to howls when he realized that I was there and Linda wasn't, but I picked him up and talked to him until he calmed down and looked me over, like he was trying to remember where he'd seen me before. I laid down with him on the double bed and played peek-a-boo behind a pillow until he broke into a grin. Then he threw back his round head and closed his eyes like a little fat man. He had a wonderful, deep belly laugh. But in the middle of our game I looked around and realized that I was in Linda and Ray's bed, with my head on their pillows.

"Come on, Jeremy," I said, sitting up suddenly, "let's get out of here and have some supper."

After he ate a little cereal, I took him down from his high chair and put him on the worn carpet in the living room, beside a plastic basket filled with toys. I piled the toys all around him, deciding that my goal would be to totally exhaust him, so that he would be asleep when Linda came home. Then she would be happy and I would feel useful, something I hadn't felt in months. I took an armload of plastic cars into the tub and ran a bath for him, and he played in the water until his fingers and toes were like prunes. He still wailed when I lifted him from the tub, but this had tired him out. All I had to do was sing a few nursery songs and waltz him around the narrow spaces between the furniture in the living room until he fell asleep against my shoulder. It was exactly eleven o'clock. I settled him into his crib, picked up the living room, and then settled on the lumpy, faded sofa with my mystery novel.

At eleven thirty Linda came home alone, tiptoeing, her face drained of color. "Is he asleep?" she whispered.

I nodded proudly. "Out like a light."

Her tired face broke into a smile. "Oh, I can't believe it!" she whispered. "I was sure I'd find him hysterical."

"He hardly cried at all," I said. "We had a great time."

"You did?" she asked, amazed.

"Everything went fine, really."

"God, I'm so relieved," Linda said. "This is *wonderful*. You have to understand, this is the first time I've ever left him with anyone. I was so nervous about it, but this party was so important to Ray. I'm so tired—I just can't stay up as late as I used to. My doctor says it's because of the C section." She said this as though I would understand. Then she took off her coat and stretched her arms over her head, yawning.

"Did Ray stay at the party?" I asked.

"Oh, he didn't want to leave. He's having the time of his life. He hasn't had a chance to fool around with his friends in ages. Tonight he'll go till he drops."

She flopped down on the sofa beside me and put her head back. "Whew," she sighed. "I'm really beat." She began rummaging in her purse for her money. "Do you like baby-sitting, Bonnie?" she asked.

"Sure," I said. "Anytime."

"Thank goodness you have your bike—I'm too tired to move." She smiled a dreamy, exhausted smile. "I'm going to take a long, hot bath all by myself."

I was glad I had made her happy. I pushed off into the night on my bicycle and thought about how different she was from Jenny. I hoped she'd be calling me again soon.

"Can you baby-sit this Saturday again?" she asked. "And did you know you forgot your book? I read it yesterday and today while Jeremy took his nap. I love mystery novels! It's the first book

33

I've read in about a year. Do you have any other good ones?"

I was thrilled. "I have dozens. What time do you want me to come on Saturday?"

"Come at six thirty again. Do you have any by that same author? And you don't have to ride your bike. Ray can pick you up."

"I don't mind," I insisted quickly. I couldn't imagine riding in the Audi with Ray.

With the same smile she watched me climb her stairs. I handed her two paperbacks.

"I think you'll like these. If you liked the other one."

"Fantastic! I was afraid you'd forget."

"Is that her?" Ray's voice thundered as we stepped into the kitchen. "I'll be ready in two seconds."

"Just give me a minute," Linda called back. "I need to tell her some stuff about Jeremy."

Ray came hurrying into the kitchen. "First find my blue windbreaker. I've looked everywhere. I'll need it on the boat." And he gave her a little push toward the bedroom. His tanned face loomed above me. He smiled blindingly. He had a headband around his forehead, and his sun-bleached hair was still wet. "Hell, I can't find anything in this shoe box," he complained, grinning. "Good thing it's summer. I get claustrophobia in here."

"It *is* small," I said. "But nice."

He shook his head, disagreeing amiably. "Me, I'd be happier living on a boat. God, I wish I had a boat. My friend Les has a great twenty footer. You like sailing?"

I nodded blankly.

"Ever been windsurfing?"

I shook my head. I actually hadn't been to the beach at all that summer. I felt suddenly unbearably pale.

Ray was still watching me, puzzled now. "Do you *like* baby-sitting?" he asked me.

"It depends on the kids," I said. "I like Jeremy."

He beamed at this answer. "Yeah, he's a great little kid, old Jeremy. I'm going to teach him how to surf. Soon as he can walk, that is." He chuckled. "I never thought I'd ever have a kid, though. You know what I mean?"

I shrugged, not sure.

"I mean, I never thought . . ." He paused, and at that moment Linda came back into the room with the blue windbreaker and a purple one for herself. "It was right where I said it was," she scolded. "In the drawer." She held up the purple windbreaker. "I might go on the boat myself tonight," she said to Ray.

To me she added softly, "I have to start keeping up with him."

He put his arm around her waist and began to pull her toward the back door. She laughed and let herself be dragged. "Cut it out, Ray! Did you tell Bonnie what to feed Jeremy?"

"Applesauce!" she called from the back landing. "In the fridge!"

"Don't worry!" I called. I heard them both laughing from the street. They roared away.

This time Linda tiptoed in at midnight. Jeremy was safely down, and I was reading. I pointed wordlessly to the bedroom, and she sighed, eased herself beside me on the sofa, and closed her eyes.

"I tried," she said. "But I practically fell asleep standing up."

"It's a little later," I reminded her. "A whole half hour."

But she shook her head and opened her eyes. "I'm wrecked. I'm wasted. I was too tired to even *dance*." She said this like I might not believe her.

"What did you do?" I asked.

"I sat in a chair!" Linda wailed. "Watching everybody else having fun. They looked at me in my chair and wondered: What happened to the old Linda Mason?"

"You're just tired from having a baby," I insisted. "My mom still gets tired, and she had her baby last summer." Then I fell silent, wondering what sense it could possibly make to compare Linda to my mother.

But Linda seemed momentarily relieved to hear this. Then her face grew long again. "People don't understand what it's like," she said, "to change so much in a year. God, I used to be able to party all night long."

"All night long?" I echoed.

"My parents never knew. I used to make up the wildest excuses. And I never got caught—not once."

"I've never stayed out all night long," I admitted. "Except for a few slumber parties."

Linda smiled. "It wasn't so different from a slumber party, what I was doing. It was just having fun, doing crazy things with my best friend. Nothing bad, just good clean fun, know what I mean?"

I nodded.

"Till I met Ray, that is," she added, and tossed back her head with a laugh. "Ray took me past the good-clean-fun stage. There were these incredible parties. And we were the couple everybody wanted at their party. Ray is such a great dancer. Oh man, we had fun."

I listened, hanging on to every word.

She sighed. "Well, Ray is happy tonight. Out in the boat with all his pals." She closed her eyes again. "Oh, Bonnie," she said softly, "never marry a guy who—"

Then she stopped and put her hand over her mouth.

"A guy who what?" I pressed.

"A guy who makes you feel crazy," Linda finished. "Have you ever met a guy who makes you feel absolutely crazy?"

I didn't know how to answer her. I felt suddenly caught out—hopelessly immature. I shrugged.

"Oh, don't listen to me. I'm a zombie." She looked down at the paperback on the sofa between us. "Hey, did you finish your book? What did you think of the ending?"

"I'm not sure if I believed it," I said. "I just couldn't accept that a fourteen-year-old boy masterminded all those murders alone."

"But he was a *genius*," Linda reminded me. "They kept stressing how much smarter he was than anyone else in the family. And he was so ambitious."

"But why would he have killed his own *grandmother*? They never really explained that. She was on his side."

"So that no one would suspect him. It was a brilliant move."

We ended up talking for almost an hour about *Grandmother's Garrote*. I was thrilled that Linda was interested. I had no one else to talk to about detective novels. My mother and father thought it was a passing, morbid phase.

"Uh-oh!" Linda exclaimed, looking at the cracked plastic clock beside the sofa. "I've kept you almost a whole extra hour. Listen, I'll pay you for it."

"You don't have to," I protested. "Please don't. I don't know anybody else who reads detective novels."

"I guess Jenny is more the *Vogue* magazine type lately, isn't she?" Linda asked.

I shrugged, wondering whether or not to tell her that I didn't really see much of Jenny anymore. But Linda had gotten up to find her purse. She counted out the money, trying again to pay me for the extra hour, but I wouldn't take it.

When I left, I said, "Tell me next time what you think of the second book."

"I will," she said. "See you Saturday!"

So I began to baby-sit for Linda every Saturday night, and sometimes during the week, all the way through June and into July, while she and Ray went to either a small or a large party, a house party or a beach party—always a party. Once in a great while she and Ray would come home together, and on those occasions, I would leave quickly. Ray was friendly, and he seemed as grateful as Linda for my success with Jeremy, but there was something about his deep voice and his easy smile and the smell of beer on his breath when he would come home that always made me want to bolt. Sometimes, as I rode my bike home through the empty streets on those summer nights, I wondered if they talked about me, about how much younger I seemed than them, how thin I was, how unwomanly I was, how I never had plans on Saturday night—these thoughts made me cringe.

But most of the time Linda left looking fantastic and came home alone, looking pale and tired and disappointed, complaining about how awful it was not to have enough energy to keep up with Ray. I could tell that she was growing uneasy about letting him stay out that much later than she did, although for my benefit she spoke about it like it was perfectly normal. So I acted like it was normal too.

She and I would sit down together at the kitchen table, and she would open a Coke for each of us and we would talk, first about Jeremy, then about detective novels and mystery movies. And then, gradually, Linda began to tell me stories of her own high-school days and about her best friend, Lou.

Lou had loved mystery novels too, and she had wanted to be a writer. Linda told me about their adventures, about how the two of them used to trade boyfriends and get crushes on the same teachers and share clothes because they were the same size. I hung on to every word, waiting for the day she would tell me what it had been like to run away with Ray. It seemed a little strange to me that she never mentioned it. Sometimes when she was going on about something she had done with Lou, I would get a strange feeling, like I had heard someone else telling me the same type of stories in the same way.

Then one night, as I was listening to her, it came to me. She was speaking about her past in the same way that my mother sometimes did—a past so distant and far away that it can sound like a story of long ago. And yet when I looked at Linda, with her thick dark hair and her eyes shining and her chin in her hands, it was like I was talking to someone my own age. We liked the same teachers. We both wore jean jackets and sweatshirts. We both loved detective novels. It was easy to forget that there was a sleeping baby in the next room and a husband coming home later, and then something would remind me, like the sight of Ray's clothes on a hook in the bathroom. It was a mystery beyond the mysteries of the books we had begun to share—the mystery of Linda's apartment, her baby, her husband, her profoundly adult life. It pulled me in.

Dear Lou,

Great news! I found a super baby-sitter. Somehow I could tell the minute I saw this girl that she would be perfect. The way she looks at Jeremy—really looks *at him, like she thinks he's wonderful—my sister hasn't ever once looked at him that way. And there's something about this girl—she's so* interested *in every single thing I say. I've missed that a lot since the old days with you. She acts like baby-sitting for Jeremy is about the most exciting thing she's ever done! She's a gold mine!*

She also reads the same kind of books you used to like—do you still read detective stories? Anyway, I'm glad I called her. I was starting to get really burned out taking care of the baby by myself all the time. I love being a mom—don't get me wrong. But you do get bored with it, day in, day out. Ray especially. He's been complaining a lot about us never going out anymore, so I think I found this girl just in time.

And now we've actually been to a couple of south-shore beach parties—you remember Les and Mickey and that whole gang? The parties are still the same—swimming, dancing, lots of booze. Ray is his old life-of-the-party self again. But I think it's going to take me a little longer to get back into the swing of things. I'm still too tired to really cut loose. Plus I'm the only one there who has a kid. There's nobody who I can talk to about it. It's kind of a weird feeling.

More soon.

Love,
Linda

FIVE

And then a boy I didn't know called me, said he was Bob Zanderwells, and asked me to go to a movie with him the next Saturday. I didn't answer right away; I was straining to remember if I knew anyone named Bob.

"Do you go to my school?" I asked.

"No, I go to Central. I know you from Mrs. Piccato's."

Mrs. Piccato was my piano teacher. The only boy my own age I knew from piano was a rather gloomy-looking one who had started taking his lessons right before mine. Mrs. Piccato called him Roberto.

"Are you Roberto?" I asked.

"Only at Mrs. Piccato's," he said. "The rest of the time, I'm Bob Zanderwells."

"Well, I have a baby-sitting job Saturday nights," I said.

"*Every* Saturday?" he asked.

I was about to quickly explain that I was available Friday nights when the voice said good-bye and hung up. I sat holding the receiver a few moments, confused. The boy I saw at Mrs. Piccato's house had never even said hello to me. He was so unfriendly that after the first few times I'd seen him, I didn't even bother looking at him. He always came out of Mrs. Piccato's parlor with his head down, like he was unhappy about how the lesson had gone.

I had a piano lesson a few days later. I went ten minutes early and waited to see if Bob Zanderwells would come out of Mrs. Piccato's parlor before I went in. At four o'clock, out he came, looking particularly glum. I looked right at his face, fully prepared now to give him a friendly hello. But he walked right past me out to the porch with his head down, climbed onto his bike, and rode away.

When Mrs. Piccato called me in for my lesson, I asked, "Was that Bob Zanderwells?"

"That's my Roberto," Mrs. Piccato corrected me.

"Is he a little shy?" I asked.

"He'll get over it," Mrs. Piccato said philosophically. "He's at *that age*." She winked.

The next day he called me again.

"Didn't you see me at Mrs. Piccato's?" I asked.

"Would you want to go to a movie on a *Friday* night?" he asked in the same somber voice.

I hesitated, asking myself, *Do I want to?* It was hard to imagine having any fun with him.

"What movie?" I asked. There was a pause.

"I'll call you back," he said.

He doesn't even have a movie in mind, I thought. I looked through the papers myself for a good one.

When he called back, I said, "Let's go see the Agatha Christie."

"Okay," he said, sounding relieved.

I waited for him to say something about how and when we would go. After another long pause I suggested, "We'll ride our bikes and go to the early movie. You could ride by around quarter of seven, okay, Bob?"

"Okay," he said again.

When I told my mother and father a boy had called me and asked me to go to a movie, they exchanged a long, intense look.

"What did you say his name was?" my dad asked, trying to sound nonchalant.

"Bob," I replied. "He takes piano from Mrs. Piccato. That's where we met."

But my mother couldn't hold back. "Bonnie, your first date!" she sang, clapping her hands. In her lap, Ben jumped in his sleep.

"It isn't a big deal," I insisted. "I don't even know if I like him. And he's really shy."

"Well, give him a chance," she said. "There's nothing wrong with being a little shy. Your father was shy." She gave him a smile.

"I was not," he protested, but he smiled, too.

"I mean *real* shy," I insisted, but then dropped it, figuring they'd see for themselves the next evening.

So when Linda called to ask me if I could baby-sit on Friday night instead of Saturday, I had to tell her I couldn't. It made me uncomfortable, like I was letting her down.

"I'm going out," I said guiltily.

"Going out!" Linda asked. "Do you have a *date*?" Then she caught herself and cried, "*Listen* to me! It's none of my *business*!"

"It's all right," I said. "I'm just going to a movie. We're going to see the Agatha Christie." I didn't want her to know it was my first real date.

"Ooooh, lucky you," she said. "I've heard that's a really good one. Who does it have in it?"

I told her, and she sighed enviously. "Well, that's

what I get for waiting till the last minute. I'll talk to you later, okay?"

"I can still sit Saturday or Sunday," I offered.

"Oh, Ray really wants to go to this one big party. There's supposed to be a band and everything. But maybe he'll go alone. I'm a little tired of his friends anyway."

I could hear Jeremy starting to cry in the background. She said good-bye and hung up, and I sat by the phone a moment, wishing it were possible to ask her to come to the movie with Bob Zanderwells and me.

Introducing Bob to my parents was an ordeal. They were making an effort to restrain their curiosity, and because of this, and because Bob was too nervous to say anything on his own, there was one excruciatingly long silence after another. Bob stood in the middle of the room with his head down and his arms crossed.

Finally my mom said, "You two don't want to be late for your movie. We'll talk later." She pushed us both out the door.

Bob followed me to the shed, where I kept my ten-speed. He seemed dazed.

"It's a Ross," I said, making conversation. "I've only had it about a month. Yours looks new too. Have you had it long?"

"No," he said.

"It looks really well made. Did you get it here in town?"

"Yes."

I asked him a few more things, questions that came easily because I had done some research on bicycles before I'd picked out mine. But he answered everything in monosyllables, staring at the spokes of his Fuji.

"Well, I hope I don't ride too fast for you," I joked. If he had at least smiled! But instead he looked like any minute he would snap to attention and salute me.

Throughout the entire movie he never looked at me. He bought me popcorn without looking at me. He slid into the aisle and sat beside me without looking at me. Halfway through the movie, he sneezed a few times.

"Bless you, Roberto," I said, trying again to be funny. When the movie was over and the credits were playing, I leaned toward him a little, so that he would have to look right into my face, and asked, "Did you like it?"

"Like what?"

"The movie!"

"Yes."

"The ending was a little weird, didn't you think?" I asked, still staring at him. He had leaned back into his seat slightly, but he nodded. His eyes darted around.

"Oh, let's go," I said, getting up.

He rode ahead of me on the way back to my house. I watched him coasting along the path that cut through the park. He was tall and thin, and his light-brown hair was blowing into a circle of curls around his head. He was actually quite handsome, but very unhappy-looking. And I had never met anyone so shy. He stopped his bike in front of my house, and I pushed my bike past him into the yard. He stood at the gate while I locked up. I was tired of trying to get him to talk.

But I said, "Do you have a lesson next week?"

He nodded.

"Well, I'll see you then, okay?"

He climbed back on his bike and rode away. It was only ten o'clock. I stood watching him, my disappointment sinking in. My first date. What a joke! From the yard I could see into the living room. My parents were watching TV. I wasn't ready to go in. I had a sudden longing to talk to a friend. Impulsively, I unlocked my bike and quietly pushed off again, into the alley and toward Baker Street.

I rode past the house first to make sure that there was no Audi in the driveway and that there were still lights on upstairs. Through the tiny kitchen window I could make out Linda's head and shoulders.

Linda heard me coming up. She opened the back door a crack and then pushed it wide. "Bonnie!" she cried. She was wearing one of Ray's huge pajama tops, holding Jeremy. "What are you doing here?"

"It was too early to go home. My date is over."

"Over already! Was it okay? Did something bad happen?"

"No, the guy I went out with had to be home early," I said. "It was fine."

"Geez, I'm so glad to *see* you! Jeremy is such a crab tonight, I can hardly stand him."

She was smiling, but I glanced at her face more closely. Her eyes were puffy. Jeremy reached for me, and I took him from her. "Are you driving your mother crazy?" I asked him, jiggling him to make him smile. His face broke into a watery grin.

"God, look at him, smiling at you like a little clown. He's done nothing but whine at me all day."

Her eyes were unmistakably red. "Are you tired?" I asked her. "I won't stay if you're tired."

"Don't you dare leave now that you've got Jeremy smiling. Sit down, right there." She pointed to the table. "Can I get you a Coke?" I nodded and sat down with Jeremy on my lap. Linda opened me a Coke and then sat down across from me, rubbing her forehead like her head was hurting.

"Are you okay?" I asked.

"Oh, I'm fine," she insisted. She hesitated and then added, "I was a little mad at Ray. But no point in both of us staying home, right?"

I didn't answer.

"Anyway, tell me about this guy you're dating. Is he cute?"

It seemed so funny to call what I had just been through a date that I grinned. Linda thought I was beaming with pride.

"He *is* cute," she gushed. "Is it serious?"

"This was the first time I ever went out with him. He's so shy he can hardly talk."

Linda nodded knowingly. "Oh, the *shy* type. Lots of uncomfortable silences, right?"

I nodded. "I tried to get him to talk, but nothing worked."

"Yeah, I dated a guy like that once. His name was *Howie*—can you stand it? He was just unbelievably shy, but handsome! He had the most incredibly beautiful brown eyes and long eyelashes out to here. Howie Bakerfield. I thought he didn't like me. Turns out he was *crazy* about me but too scared to do anything about it. He told me all of this a year later, when we were both dating other people. So I almost *never* knew!

"I think this guy might be just as shy," I said, thrilled that she knew what it was like.

"Oh, I'll bet this guy likes you a *lot*, Bonnie. It sounds to me like all he can handle right now is getting up the nerve to go out at all."

"Maybe you're right," I agreed in a hushed voice. Then Linda looked away off over my head, thinking. Her smile grew distant too. "Oh god, but that Ray," she said softly. "He sure wasn't shy. I was the shy one with Ray. At first, I mean. I used to get completely unglued before a date with Ray. Couldn't eat, couldn't sleep, didn't want to talk to anybody else. I'd never felt like that before. And sometimes he'd forget to call me, and it would be like the end of the *world*. Oh, everything was different with Ray. I wanted to change my whole life after I met him. I wanted to feel . . . to feel . . ."

"To feel what?" I blurted, and Linda looked up, startled out of her thoughts, and saw that against my chest, Jeremy's head was dropping and his eyes were rolling up into his head. He was desperately fighting sleep.

Linda started giggling. I tried not to. "Don't make me laugh," I pleaded. "I'll wake him up."

"Go to sleep, you little monster," Linda whispered. "Give us a break."

After a moment he started to snore. Linda ran ahead to the bedroom, pulling the blanket back on his bed as I slid him in. "Oh, if he wakes up now, I'll *die*," Linda groaned.

But he didn't wake up, and we both stood looking down at him.

"You sure are a great baby-sitter," Linda said. "Jeremy is crazy about you."

"I'm just used to taking care of a baby," I said, "because of my little brother." But it wasn't because of Ben. Ben was very normal and well tended. Jeremy seemed a much more interesting, complex baby to me—more of a character. He often had a slightly ironic expression on his face—not like a baby's at all, as if he had figured out that he was the product of extreme action and uncontrollable feelings. I felt needed by him.

Linda and I tiptoed out. When my eyes suddenly fell on Ray's kimono spread across the bed, I jumped. I was suddenly uncomfortable. "I think I'd better go home now," I said to Linda. "My parents are expecting me."

Linda looked disappointed. She glanced at the clock on the wall. "Ray is probably just getting started," she grumbled.

"You said you didn't want to go to that party," I reminded her.

"Oh, I didn't at first. But when Ray started getting ready, like he just couldn't wait to get out of here, it really got to me."

I felt a rush of sympathy. "If you wanted him to stay home, he should have," I said.

But Linda shook her head, disagreeing. "No, it's better if he goes. He needs to see his friends."

At the door she managed a smile. "It was so sweet of you to come over like this. Do it anytime, please?" She hugged me.

My mom was still up when I came in. She noticed that I was smiling to myself. She patted the sofa beside her and, when I sat down, put an arm around my shoulders.

"You look happy," she said. "Have a nice date?"

I had almost completely forgotten it. "Well, it wasn't easy," I said. "He's terribly shy. But I tried to be friendly. I think all he can handle is getting up the nerve to go out at all."

My mother's eyebrows rose in approval. "You're probably absolutely right," she said. "And maybe it'll go better next time."

I nodded and stood up. Before I left the room, I said, "I really like Jenny's sister, Linda, Mom. And she says I'm a great baby-sitter."

My mother listened to this thoughtfully. "I'm glad it's working out," she said quietly. "I'm sure Linda is grateful to have a baby-sitter who's a friend of the family. Is Jenny back yet?"

"Back from where?"

"Back in town. You said she was out of town."

"Oh, she is," I said, remembering. "I'm . . . waiting for her to call me. It's her turn."

Now my mother looked slightly troubled. She bit her lip. "Can I just say one more thing?" she asked.

I sighed.

"Do you think Jenny might possibly be upset because you're baby-sitting for her sister? You know how sensitive she's been about all that."

I rolled my eyes. "If she is, Mom, it's just too bad. Was I supposed to ask her permission?"

"Are you and Jenny fighting?" she asked, shifting gears.

I didn't answer.

"Answer me, Bonnie—did you have a falling out with Jenny?"

"Mom, it wasn't just one fight. All we ever did was argue. It wasn't just about Linda. We're really different, Mom."

"Everyone is different."

"Mom, you know what I mean."

"I'm not sure I *do* know what you mean," she insisted softly. "But I don't want to argue about this tonight. Tonight was a special night for you. I just want you to know that I am disappointed about you and Jenny. For your sake. I'm concerned about the way you push people aside when they're not exactly who you want them to be."

"Mom—"

"No, no, that's all I'm going to say. For now. Go to bed." And she blew me a weary kiss.

"Good night," I called crossly, wishing she hadn't brought up Jenny at all.

Dear Lou,

I guess you must be pretty busy getting ready for college, right? College seems far away from me now, but I hope it goes really well for you. Did you decide to go into journalism like you used to talk about? I still think I probably would have gone into some kind of social work. Remember how everyone was always telling me that I would be great working with people? It's kind of strange to think about now, isn't it? Here I am with my own little family. And you so far away!

Thank heavens I have this baby-sitter. One thing I can't for the life of me figure out is how this girl puts up with Jenny. They're complete opposites! My baby-sitter has this boyfriend, and he's so shy she can't even get him to talk to her. Remind you of anyone?

She's got a lot to learn about boys—I'm trying to fill her in a little.

Ray and I have still been going out a lot, but the last few times we've been to the south beach, I just end up feeling out of it. Sometimes I leave early, just 'cause I'm bored. Ray doesn't understand—he stays practically till morning and then he comes home and wants to jump all over me. He says how come I'm always so tired and why am I turning into such a wet blanket. Then I remember you and me roaring around in your car at all hours, and I say, "You don't even know what fun is, Ray! You should have seen me in the old days!"

Will you please *write soon? It is your turn, you know.*

Love,
Linda

SIX

Robert's Fuji was parked in Mrs. Piccato's yard. A couple of paperbacks were clamped into the carrier on his fender. I glanced at them quickly, wanting to know what he read—maybe it would help start a conversation. One of the books was a biography of Mozart. The other, to my amazement, was a copy of *The Maltese Falcon*, by Dashiell Hammett. I had read it a dozen times.

I rehearsed how I would ask him what he thought of it when his lesson ended. Unexpectedly, Mrs. Piccato came out first, and while she greeted me, I heard the faint sounds of someone leaving her house through the back door. I ran to the window just in time to see Bob Zanderwells pull his Fuji into the street.

"You look pretty today, Bonita," Mrs. Piccato said. "Your haircut is just darling."

Somehow I managed to sputter through my piano lesson. *You blew it,* I berated myself. *He's too shy and you were too impatient.*

But then he called me the next evening. I was so surprised, I forgot to be gentle. "Go to the movies!" I exclaimed. "You wouldn't even say hello to me yesterday!"

Silence. Then he cleared his throat and said, "I was nervous. Do you want to see another movie with me or not?"

"I'll go with you if you promise to talk to me a little."

"Okay," he agreed.

"Well?" I asked.

"Well, what?"

"What time do you want to *go*?"

"I'll ride by at two thirty." He hung up abruptly, without even telling me what movie we were going to see.

"Ask him how he likes his piano lessons," Linda suggested. "Ask him if he has any brothers or sisters."

"But I can't just ask him one question after another! He has to ask *me* something too."

"Hey, he will. Trust me. It'll just take him a little longer."

I thought about the Hammett book again and made a mental note to bring it up.

"You might just be surprised about him," Linda said knowingly. "Maybe he'll turn out to be a real tiger."

We went into the bedroom together to check on Jeremy. He was dreaming of something that was making him smile.

"I've kept you late again, haven't I?" Linda whispered. She had come home alone and made us each an ice cream sundae. She said there was nobody at the party sober enough to talk to.

"Why don't you just tell Ray that you don't want to go to those kinds of parties anymore?" I asked her. "You don't seem to have fun at them."

"At least it gets me out of the house."

"Why don't you go somewhere else then, like with a friend?"

"My friends have all moved away," she answered quietly. "Besides, I have to keep an eye on Ray. Other girls get ideas. . . ." She shrugged.

"I don't see how you're doing that, always coming home early," I insisted.

Linda looked uncomfortable. After a moment, she said, "Well, you have to have a little trust, too." She licked chocolate from her spoon, and her eyes got dreamy. "God, we had fun that first summer," she said. "Ray used to make me laugh. He was always full of himself and I was so proud of him. I thought once we started going to parties, it would feel that way again."

"But it doesn't?" I asked bluntly.

She looked more matter-of-fact. "All couples have their ups and downs," she said. "You'll understand what I mean when you're married."

"I know," I said, trying to sound like I did.

"I'm not going to ask him to come in this time," I explained to my parents before Bob Zanderwells was due to arrive. "I'm hoping it will make him less nervous."

"Good strategy," my dad agreed. He seemed relieved. My mom said, "There'll be plenty of time to get to know him once he knows *you* better."

We were leaving the movie house a few hours later, walking our bikes along the sidewalk, when he asked, "Should we get something to eat?"

"Okay," I agreed. "Let's try the Dairy Isle."

He asked me what I was hungry for and what I liked on my hot dog and a few other questions—

I could see that he was really trying. He was wearing a Save the Whales T-shirt and baggy white shorts, and he was getting a tan.

"Have you been going to the beach a lot, Roberto?" I asked, trying for a conversation.

"No," he replied. "My dad has a pool. And why do you keep calling me Roberto?"

"I don't know. It fits you."

"Why?"

I shrugged. "Because you're kind of . . . serious." I'd been about to say *strange*. "But if you don't like it, I'll call you Bob."

"I'm not always serious," he insisted quietly. "I just get nervous sometimes, and then I can't think of anything to say. Especially around girls."

"People can still say hello when they're nervous. You didn't even look at me at Mrs. Piccato's."

He took a deep breath and blurted, "That's because I watched you coming down the street on your bike through the window in her parlor, and it got me so nervous I completely screwed up the end of my lesson."

I looked at him, surprised.

"Your hair was different," he added. Then he blushed and turned his attention to his food. I felt amazed. And I didn't want to lose the impetus of our first meaningful conversation.

"I saw that you were reading *The Maltese Falcon*," I said quickly. "I love Hammett."

"I know," he said.

"You *know*?"

"You were reading a couple of his books a month ago. Before your music lesson. So I got this one from the library." He lifted his head again. "You think I don't look at you, but I do."

We were both a bit overwhelmed. We didn't say another word to each other all the way back to my house, but before I took my bike into the yard, I asked, "When I see you at Mrs. Piccato's, will you still ignore me, Roberto?"

He gave me the first smile I had ever seen on his face, a smile that was both shy and relieved, with a little curve at one side.

"Do you want me to stop calling you Roberto?" I asked him again.

"Call me Robert," he said.

I couldn't wait to tell Linda. But when I got to her apartment, she was pacing the apartment, her face tense. Ray wasn't around. "He went out to put gas in the car two hours ago," she said. "He *still* hasn't come back."

I had never before seen her angry. Her face was pinched and her eyes fierce. I didn't know what to do. "He'll probably be back any minute," I mumbled.

Jeremy was in his high chair. He began to whine.

"Come on, Jeremy," I soothed, pulling him out of his chair.

"Oh, hell, where *is* he?" Linda cried at the kitchen window. She turned and watched me jiggling Jeremy. "You're glad to see Bonnie, aren't you, Jeremy?" she crooned. And to me, "You know, he's not friendly like this with just anyone. He could care less about Jenny. Of course she doesn't give him the time of day. Why do you think she's so turned off to babies?"

"She thinks she's above all that," I said, but then I was sorry. After all, they were sisters.

Just at that moment Jeremy reached for the edge of the table and grabbed the bottle Linda had been making for him, spilling juice all down his front. He leaned away from me, covering his face with his hands. Linda and I both started to laugh. Jeremy threw back his head and laughed with us.

"You little rat," Linda laughed, taking him from me and pulling off his soaked T-shirt. I mopped up the juice with a sponge. Suddenly we heard the sound of footsteps on the stairs. "Speaking of rats," Linda said softly. When Ray threw the door open, he looked at us, bewildered by all the giggling he'd heard. I picked Jeremy up and took him into the living room.

"What was so funny?" I heard Ray ask.

"Where have you been?" Linda cried. "You've been gone since four o'clock!"

"I told you I needed to run some errands," Ray insisted. "Will you just lay off of me!"

"You can go to hell!" Linda cried. I cringed, bouncing Jeremy to distract him. But when Ray stomped out the door again, she ran past me to find her windbreaker. Her face was frantic. Jeremy struggled in my arms and wailed for her as she ran past again. But she seemed to have forgotten us. We heard her running down the stairs, and Jeremy put his head against my chest, sniffling in defeat.

"It's okay, Jeremy," I said. "We'll have fun, don't worry."

But it took me longer than ever to cheer him up. It was all Ray's fault. I had a feeling that Linda would be more discouraged than usual when she came home again. But I would be ready to cheer her up too, with my good news about Robert.

"I told you he really liked you!" Linda exclaimed. "He sounds more and more like the guy I was telling you about—Howie Bakerfield—so shy he wouldn't call for days, and naturally I thought he couldn't care less about me when all the while—"

"And on Thursday," I interrupted, "he waited for me after his piano lesson, and then we rode home together on our bikes. We talked about music. We like some of the same composers."

"Composers! Come on!" she teased. "And does this mean you won't be available anymore on Saturday nights?"

"I'll still baby-sit," I assured her. "I really like having someone to talk to about this stuff."

"Don't you and Jenny talk about it?"

I wanted her to know about Jenny and me. "I actually don't see much of her lately," I said. "We aren't very close anymore."

"What happened?"

"I guess we grew apart," I said lamely. I didn't see how I could really explain it to Linda.

"Grew apart? What do you mean, grew apart? You two are too young to grow apart. Did you have a fight?"

"Jenny has some new friends," I said. "From other schools."

Linda frowned. "What is she, hanging around all the time with those prep-school kids? Getting a big head?"

I said I didn't know.

She shook her head. "Well, you may have noticed that I'm not very close to her either. We never were—too different, I guess. But I thought you two had a really nice friendship. You shouldn't let things pull you apart. Jenny will be sorry. I should know."

I wanted to protest that I didn't even miss Jenny, but when I looked closely at Linda, I saw that her eyes had filled with tears. She was blinking them back, trying to control them.

"Friends should stick by each other," she said softly.

Dear Lou,

When I asked you to please write, I sure didn't mean a letter like that last one. I need letters like that like I need a hole in the head. I'm sorry if my life doesn't seem up to your standards. And what do you mean, Ray has to change? Since when are you an expert on my husband? What were you implying with those remarks about the south-shore crowd? Were you including Ray? Do you expect me to go along with you every time you insult my husband?

And I didn't say I was bored with my life in my last letter, Lou—I said I was tired. *There's a big difference. My baby-sitter says lots of women are tired for a whole year after they have a C section. She doesn't see it as some kind of failure. She doesn't assume I'm a complete social reject because I'm still in St. Martins.*

71

She doesn't insult my husband every time she mentions him. She's practically still a child, but at least she knows that much.

I thought I could confide in you without getting insulted in return. But if you're going to put down Ray and his friends every time you write to me, then maybe you should just forget it! Send your letters to somebody who likes to be put down. I don't need it.

Maybe the problem is that you're jealous because you've never had with a man what I have with Ray. Maybe when you meet somebody yourself, we'll be able to talk again. I don't know. I'm tired of your bitchy letters. I almost feel like giving up.

Linda

SEVEN

Robert had told me very little about his parents, but I tried to be patient. He lived alone with his father; his mother taught English at a college in Minneapolis. It was hard to arrange conversations when we were both on our bikes so much, but sometimes we would stop and walk them, stretching out our time together.

Mostly, I talked and Robert listened. I told him about my family and how caught up my parents were with Ben. I also told him about my disappointing friendship with Jenny—about the way she had changed when her sister had run away. While I was explaining this, Robert interrupted me.

"I remember all that," he said. "About those

two who just disappeared. It was in the paper, wasn't it? I was shocked when I read about it."

"Well, you might have gotten the wrong impression about Jenny's sister from the papers," I insisted quickly. "Linda is a wonderful person."

"How do you know?"

"I baby-sit for her every Saturday."

"Is *that* who you baby-sit for?"

I nodded proudly.

"Isn't it a little strange to baby-sit for somebody so young, who . . . who . . ."

"No, I really like her," I said. "And Jeremy— her baby—he's a great little kid."

"To go off like that," Robert was saying, "and then end up having a *baby*. It just seems so . . . extreme. Did she ever tell you why she did it?"

I didn't want to admit that she hadn't. "I guess it was just something she had to do," I said.

Robert was shaking his head. It didn't surprise me that he didn't understand. He had never met Linda. And he was too unlike her and Ray—too serious.

Sometimes I wished we laughed and joked around more. But Robert still could hardly manage to look directly at me. I was beginning to really like *his* looks, though. He was wearing his hair longer and combing it back. And he had beautiful hands—broad but with long, thin fingers. Not that I'd ever held hands with him. We were always riding or walking our bikes.

One afternoon we waited for each other during our piano lessons. I listened to Robert's lesson from Mrs. Piccato's parlor and he waited on her front steps, listening to mine. When my lesson was over, I peeked at him through the parlor window. He was sitting with his chin in his hands, looking off, waiting for me to come out. I felt lucky to have him waiting. But I wondered what exactly he felt toward me. He saw me in the window and stood up.

"How did I sound?" I asked him, coming out.

He climbed onto his bike and rocked back and forth on it, searching for words. "Oh, you sounded . . . you sounded . . ."

"Wonderful?" I suggested. I was always finishing sentences for him.

He nodded.

"Mrs. Piccato asked me if you were waiting for me," I told him.

"Did you tell her I was?" he asked anxiously.

"I told her we were just friends," I said.

He looked first relieved, then unmistakably hurt.

"Why did you tell her that?" he asked. "That's what people say when they're not . . . they're not . . ."

"Serious?" I asked. I pulled my bike beside his, trying to read his face.

"When they're not serious," he repeated. He was trying to read mine.

"Robert, if I told her anything else," I said, "she would tease you about it. You know how she is."

He considered this, then smiled to himself. "Right," he said. "That's right. She would tease me." His smile deepened. We pushed off together.

We were walking our bikes after a long evening ride when Robert told me that he always spent the month of August with his mother in Minneapolis.

"The month of August?" I said. "Robert, August starts Friday!"

"I know," he said mournfully. "I'm leaving tomorrow."

"But why didn't you tell me *sooner*?"

He shrugged. "I didn't want to think about it."

I was terribly disappointed—I was getting used to having him around. For the past two weeks we had seen each other almost every day. "Do you *want* to go?" I asked him.

He shrugged. "I don't know." He cleared his throat. "I'll probably . . . I'll probably . . ."

"Miss me?" I finished. I wondered: *Who'll be your interpreter?* "Is August the only time you see your mom?" I asked him.

He nodded. "I used to live with her. Till I was twelve."

"When did your parents get divorced?"

"When I was nine."

He looked like he wanted me to ask more, so I said, "Was it pretty bad?"

"It was hard," he answered. "Not as bad as some kids have it, though. No screaming fights or anything. But I wouldn't want to ever go through it again."

"Do you have a good time when you visit your mom?"

"My mom's okay," he said quietly. "It was hard for her when I decided to live with my dad. When I go there, I try to be nice to her."

I couldn't imagine that that would be hard for him. I had come to depend on his niceness. The fact that he was leaving sank in, making me sad.

"Will you write to me?" I asked.

He looked a little surprised. "I'm actually not much of a letter writer," he said.

"Well, just send me postcards, then," I grumbled. I was frustrated, realizing that this was our good-bye. Robert wasn't even looking at me. *How is he going to remember what I look like?* I wondered.

"Robert," I asked him abruptly, "what color eyes do I have?"

"Dark blue," he said immediately. "Sometimes they look green. And you have really long eyelashes."

I laughed, surprised.

"I like your eyes," he said without looking at them. He said he'd be back at the end of August. Then he looked up at me, sighed, and looked down again. He seemed to be waiting for something to happen. It occurred to me that we should kiss—I wanted to. But our bikes were between us!

"Well, good-bye then," I said, giving up. I climbed on my bike and gave him a final wave.

He waved back, looking just as disappointed.

The following Saturday I hurried to Linda's. But when I got to the top of the stairs, it was Ray who opened the door and waved me inside. He was wearing a jacket and a tie with his faded jeans, and his sun-bleached hair was combed. He looked like a movie star.

"We're a class act tonight," he said. He pointed to himself. "Pretty jazzy, huh?"

"Nice," I said. "Where's Linda?"

She came out of the bedroom, wearing a strapless black dress. I had never seen her in a dinner dress. She looked incredibly elegant.

"Check on Jeremy, Ray," she coaxed. When he left the room, she whispered that they were going out to a restaurant for dinner, just the two of them. She raised her eyebrows at me knowingly, as though I would understand that this was some sort of victory.

Ray came up behind us with Jeremy in his arms. "One big guy, just woke up, ready to have fun," he said, holding Jeremy at arms' length awkwardly. He always held Jeremy that way, like he was afraid he'd drop him. Jeremy reached for me and wrapped his sticky arms around my neck.

"We'll both be home around midnight," Linda said.

I nodded. I watched them through the living-room window. Ray had his gigantic arm around Linda's thin shoulders, and he kissed the side of her neck as they walked to the car. She laughed, put an arm around his waist, and dropped her head back so that he could kiss her on the mouth. I thought of Robert, leaving me without even the briefest hug.

And I knew that when Linda and Ray came home, I would have to rush off and get out of their way. I wouldn't get to talk to Linda at all, about Robert or anything else. Jeremy seemed to sense my disappointment; he looked at my face, put his head on my shoulder and patted me with his little hand.

I was mixed up and sad all the next day. I stayed in my room. *Why do I even miss Robert?* I wondered. *We aren't even a real couple.* But I missed him terribly. And I had this odd, sinking feeling whenever I thought about Linda. I was worried about her, but I wasn't sure why.

On Monday I walked by her apartment after supper, wanting to see her. The Audi was gone and the lights were on. Linda opened the door a crack and then swung it wide.

"I'm so glad to see you!" she cried. "Hey, look who's here, Jeremy! Come on in, sit down, hurry up. We never got to talk on Saturday night, did we? After Ray and I had our big date." Her voice was sarcastic. "Our big date after which *he* went back to the beach. Are you hungry? Would you like a sandwich? How's everything going with that new boyfriend of yours?"

"He's gone on a trip," I replied sadly. "For the rest of the summer."

"Oh no! How could he? And you probably miss him like crazy! What a creep! Has he written you a letter yet?"

"No, but he promised he would. It's only been a few days."

"Oh, man, it's so nice to get letters from boys," she sighed. "There's nothing quite like it."

"Did Ray write you letters?" I asked.

"Oh, *him*," she scoffed. "He never had the chance. We were never apart long enough."

She shook her head, then looked back at me. "I'll bet your boyfriend writes romantic, sexy letters. Those quiet types always have a lot of feeling inside."

"Do you really think so?"

She nodded knowingly. "I dated this guy once—Alan Delaney—he wore his hair in a ponytail, and he used to send me poetry whenever he went away. I mean actual poetry that he wrote *himself*! Those poems were incredible! He was really quiet too, but oh those letters!"

She went on for a while, comparing Alan Delaney with Howie Bakerfield. "But the truth is, nothing much ever came of either one of those relationships. I always felt like there was something missing. I wanted to be just . . . overwhelmed. Completely overwhelmed. Do you feel that way about your boyfriend?"

I wasn't ready for this question. "Oh, I don't know," I mumbled.

"Do you absolutely *love* the way he kisses?" She

giggled. "I guess you must, the way you two always go to movies."

"Well, sort of," I said. I couldn't have admitted the truth. I didn't want her to think that my summer romance was so pitiful. I knew well enough that compared to Ray's bathrobe on the bed, it was nothing.

"I'd love to meet your boyfriend when he comes back," she said.

"Oh, you will," I said. And I meant it. Maybe Robert would like her once he met her. Maybe we could all be friends.

EIGHT

Ten days passed without a letter. It was disheartening. I started to feel like maybe the Robert I knew didn't even exist—maybe I had made him up. I decided to unmake him up and stop thinking about him. I quit holding my breath when I saw the mailman. I stopped riffling through the mail for a card from him. But it put me in a sorry, deflated mood.

Then Linda called on a Saturday afternoon and told me there was no need for me to baby-sit. Her voice was harsh. "Ray's going to one of his parties," she said. "Jeremy has a terrible cold, and Ray's going to just go without me again."

"Could I just come over and help you with Jeremy?" I asked. "Not like a job or anything."

"You mean, just to visit?"

"If you want."

"You really would?" She sounded on the verge of tears. "Jeremy really does have a cold, Bonnie. His nose is running like a faucet. Are you sure?"

"Course I'm sure. I'll just be staying home otherwise."

"Hey, maybe there's even a good detective movie on channel nine we could watch on our new TV," Linda said hopefully. "I'll check the *TV Guide*."

"What time should I come?"

"Come around nine. I'll order a pizza. I'll make popcorn. Maybe Jeremy'll conk out early—"

"I'll help you get him to sleep, too—don't worry."

"Oh, Bonnie," she sighed. "You're a lifesaver."

I was feeding Jeremy his cereal, while Linda made popcorn for the late movie on her tiny two-burner stove. "Actually, Robert hasn't written me at all," I confessed. "Not one single letter."

Linda jiggled the pot around over the burner, thinking. "He's intimidated," she announced with authority. "He's never written letters to a girl before."

"But he *promised* me he'd write. Maybe he's forgotten all about me."

"You're wrong," Linda insisted. "He's crazy about you. Some boys just can't write letters. He'll

84

call you when he gets back, and then you can give him hell."

She poured the popcorn into a bowl and salted it. "He *will* call you," she said, smiling. "I'd put money on it, if I had any. And then you probably won't want to baby-sit Saturday nights for me anymore."

"I will *too*."

It was comforting to hear her sounding that sure. And Jeremy was thrilled to have us both paying attention to him. He forgot about his cold and sat laughing in his high chair, shaking his head and clapping his hands to the music on the radio. Whenever a good song came on, Linda would turn it up loud, and we would take turns dancing around him, bumping into things in the tiny kitchen. We wore him out this way; he fell asleep on my lap with his blanket at ten thirty. It was a special triumph because there was a good detective movie coming on at eleven.

"God, this was a great idea!" Linda said. "I'm sure glad I'm not hanging out with a bunch of drunks at the beach."

"I've seen this movie before," I told her. "It's classic—you'll love it."

We both loved it. There was a melodramatic good-bye scene between the hero and the heroine at the end, and we cried over it, giggling at each other's tears.

"God, you're as big a sucker as me," Linda said. "Lou and I always cried at movies. Our boyfriends refused to take us to anything but Eddie Murphy movies."

"You mean Ray?"

"Oh God no, before Ray. Lou and I never double-dated after I met Ray." She sighed. "My dates with Ray just weren't the sort of dates where you bring somebody else along, if you know what I mean."

"Where is your friend Lou now?" I asked.

Linda's face hardened. "She's in Oregon."

"Did she stay in touch with you?"

"I guess she can't be bothered." Then her face changed again, grew sad. "It was never the same with us after Ray and I ran away. We ran away, you know. Did you hear all about that?"

I nodded. "A few things. From Jenny."

Linda's eyebrows rose. "From Jenny? God, her version must have been interesting."

"Actually Jenny wouldn't talk about it," I said. But then, because I felt more than ever that we were really becoming close, I added, "I've always wondered what really happened when you and Ray did that."

"What really happened, eh?" Linda said. She

sighed. "Boy, just about everything you can imagine happened on *that* trip."

"I mean, where did you *go*? What was it like? Were you traveling around the whole time?"

Linda's face drooped as she remembered. She looked off over my head. "Lou was the only person who knew where we were. She was the only one I wrote to. I thought that would mean a lot to her, but I guess I was wrong."

But I didn't want to hear about Lou. I had waited so long with my questions. "Where did you go?" I repeated.

She sighed again. "South. Through Ohio. We stayed a week in a motel, and then we—"

"In a motel?"

She nodded. "In the middle of nowhere. Then we went all the way to the Keys."

"The Keys! That far? Where did you stay there?"

Her voice dropped to almost a whisper. "Oh, Ray bought a tent. And a stove and a cooler. We were living on the beach."

"You were *living* on the beach?" I asked. It was more exotic than anything I'd imagined before.

Linda was still nodding to herself. Then her voice changed; she was suddenly upset. "See, the running away wasn't what bothered Lou. She wasn't like that—she was all for breaking the rules and having adventures. But when she found out I was pregnant and that we got married—well, *that* was what did it. Lou always said she'd never get married. But I never used to say that, Bonnie. I didn't plan to get married so young, but I never went along with that I'll-never-get-married stuff. She thought we both felt the same way about it, but we didn't."

Suddenly Linda was crying, her face in her hands. "I guess she doesn't want an old married hag for a best friend anymore," she sobbed.

"You're not an old married hag," I protested. "God, how can you even *say* that?"

Linda lifted her head. "You're such a nice kid, Bonnie."

"I'm not a *kid*," I insisted. "And you're not a hag. Being a mother doesn't make you a hag. Geez, why do you talk like that?"

"I don't know what's the matter with me," Linda said, wiping her eyes. "I'm so confused. Maybe because everything changed so fast. I was in high school having a great time, and then I met Ray and things got even better, and then bloowey—I became this old, worn-out person who can't even go to parties and have fun anymore."

"We're having fun," I reminded her, but she didn't hear.

"I'm so confused," she repeated. "I don't know what's the matter with me lately."

I didn't know what to say. Finally, I mumbled lamely, "Gee, things aren't so bad."

Then, unexpectedly, someone banged on the back door, making us both jump. "It's Ray," Linda said under her breath. She scowled at the door. The pounding grew louder.

"Aren't you going to get it?" I whispered, shocked.

At last she stood up. When she opened the door, Ray was glaring down at her.

"What's wrong?" she said coldly. "Did they run out of beer?"

I wished I could hide. I stood up.

"Hey wait," he said, stumbling in. "Don't get up, Bonnie, don't get up. Are you two having some girl talk or what?"

He lowered his weight clumsily into the chair across the table from me. I looked at Linda, but she was looking away. "Maybe I can finally learn something about *women* tonight," he said. "Bonnie probably has some advice for me, don't you?" He put his big arms on the table and waited, his eyes narrowing.

"Stop it, Ray," Linda said darkly. The tone of her voice made him turn, but I couldn't see the look they exchanged.

"I have to go now," I said. Linda followed me to the landing. I looked up at her from the bottom stair—she looked so small and unhappy. I wanted to ask her if it was okay for me to leave her with Ray, but I didn't even know what I was asking or if I had any business asking it.

She called down to me softly, "He's just a little drunk, honey. Sorry if he embarrassed you."

I waved up at her, then rode home in a daze, my face burning. I was angry. For the first time I realized that something was happening in that apartment, something that was hurting Linda. It was all Ray's fault. I wanted to help. But what could I do?

Dear Lou,

This is the last letter I'll ever write you, so don't worry, you don't even have to answer it. You don't even have to take time out from your hot-shot schedule and sit down for ten minutes and write me the latest insults you've dreamed up about my apparently too-boring-for-you life. Don't bother. If anyone had ever told me two years ago that my friend Lou would be the person who would let me down this way, the person who would insult me and be jealous of me because of her own problems with men, I never in a million years would have believed it. I would have said, "You don't know my friend Lou." I would have defended you the same way you haven't defended me. I get more respect from my fifteen-year-old baby-sitter than I get from a fifteen-year-old friendship! And if you had done the same thing I did and things were the other way around, I would have respected whatever life you chose. Because that's what real friends do. And furthermore, I can't believe that now I can't even tell you my problems. I can't confide in you, and even though I know everybody has problems and everybody has ups and downs, I can't tell you mine because you have refused from day one to treat my marriage with respect. I hope in the future you figure out for yourself what friendship really means so that you never hurt another person the way you've hurt me.

Linda

NINE

All at once I could see clearly how much Linda had changed. Her tan had faded and she had grown too thin. Her hollow cheeks made her eyes look even more intense and anxious. Her hair was longer, and she pinned it carelessly to the top of her head and it fell out little by little throughout the day. She was distracted and absentminded about Jeremy—always forgetting where she had put his clothes or his toys. She would ask me where his things were and then be surprised when I didn't know. And she started calling him her poor baby and her poor little kid.

Sometimes he would point to the window and babble. And Linda would respond, "No one is coming, poor baby."

"I think he just wants to go out," I said after I had heard this too many times.

"Out?"

"Out. Around the block. Out of the house for a while."

She looked amazed. "Is that what you've been trying to tell me?" she asked Jeremy.

"We could take him out for a walk now," I suggested.

"Oh, would you mind taking him yourself?" she pleaded. "I'm a little tired."

She was always tired—she seemed to be fading away. She had no energy for anything. She hadn't cleaned her apartment in weeks. When I tried to help her, to put something away, she'd say, "Leave that, just leave it—I'll do it tomorrow." But then she wouldn't.

I knew because I was seeing her nearly every day. I wanted to help her. I felt that the old Linda was somewhere just beneath the surface of this tired person. And I still needed her. I still wanted to be close to her, that other Linda, the one who had done reckless, incredible things.

And I wanted to know where Ray was. I had told her about Robert. I waited for her to explain Ray's absence. It seemed to me that he couldn't have gone far—too much of him was still all around us: his clothes, his sandals, his tapes in a stack beside their bed.

Linda asked me if I'd heard anything from Robert.

"Nothing," I said for the hundredth time. "Not one word."

Again she reassured me. "When he comes back, he'll apologize for days. And he'll have a million excuses."

I took a chance and said, "It'll be nice for you when Ray comes back too. From his trip."

"What trip?" Linda asked, stricken. She looked like she was afraid I knew something she didn't.

"I thought maybe he'd gone on a trip," I explained, embarrassed to have guessed wrong.

"Oh, right," she said, recovering. "I guess you could say he's on a trip." She lowered her head.

"Linda, where is he?" I asked.

"Ray needed some time to himself," she explained, lifting her chin, "so he's living on his friend Les' boat. For a few weeks." Then she looked away again.

I made myself ask, "Does he ever come here, like at night?"

Now she looked exasperated. "Well, of course he does," she insisted. "All the time."

"That's good," I said, but I didn't mean it, because I didn't believe her. For as I watched Linda change, I imagined Ray changing too, growing bigger and louder and stronger on the boat, away from the apartment he had left her in. A feeling that had taken root earlier in the summer began to grow. What was happening was all his fault. I hated him, but also wished for Linda's sake that he would come back soon.

I didn't bring it up again. Instead, I resolved to keep helping Linda, to cheer her up in the ways I had learned earlier in the summer. I took Jeremy for walks and then reported to her all the funny things he did. Linda seemed to need to hear me talk about Jeremy, now that she was too tired to deal with him herself.

We still talked about detective novels too, but only because Linda still wanted to, for now I thought the way she was reading them was strange—reading them instead of going out for walks, instead of cleaning her house, instead of playing with Jeremy. And she was always getting one book confused with another, forgetting which book had which plot or which characters. She would often ask me to remind her how a book she had just finished had ended.

And then Linda would ask me if I had yet heard from Robert, and I would have to say no, because I hadn't, and she would tell me again that I would soon. And this would start her off on one of her own stories about high school, about Lou and Howie Bakerfield and Alan Delaney and the other boyfriends, and her face would take on a dreamy expression, a look that troubled me now, although it was better than seeing her so unhappy.

My mother noticed all the time I was spending at Linda's. It was making her nervous.

"I think it's wonderful that you're being such a help," she said. "But don't you get tired of being around someone so much older?"

"She's not that much older," I said. "Besides, I'm her baby-sitter. What difference does it make if she's older?"

"And where is Robert lately?"

"He's still out of town."

"Is he really out of town? You wouldn't hand me a line about this, would you, Bonnie?"

"He *is* still out of town. I miss him like crazy."

"Is that why you're spending so much time at Linda's?"

"Oh, partly," I said. "She's having some trouble with her marriage. I'm trying to help."

My mother's brow furrowed deeper. She thought for a minute, and then she said, "Honey, are you sure you want to get involved in something like that?"

"Do you mean," I suggested, "that I should dump Linda because she has a problem?"

My mother bit her lip and didn't answer.

I was playing on the floor with Jeremy. Linda had fallen asleep on the sofa. The telephone rang—the sound startled us both. I had never heard Linda's phone ring before. At the second ring, Linda sat up and covered her face, like the very sound was too much for her.

"Don't worry," I said. "I'll get it." I picked up the receiver. "Pastrovitch residence," I said hesitantly.

"Is that you, Bonnie?" a familiar voice asked. It was Jenny. "What are you doing over there?"

"Baby-sitting," I said. *It's Jenny,* I mouthed to Linda. She rolled her eyes.

"Baby-sitting *now*?" Jenny asked. "Where is Linda?"

"Well, actually . . . she just came home. Here she is." And I handed the phone to Linda.

Linda's voice was curt. "Yes, she's my baby-sitter. Well, you never *asked*, did you? Is that my fault? Of course Ray isn't here, it's three o'clock, he's working. No, I can't come tomorrow, I have plans. Tell Mom I'll call her. All right, just a minute." She held the phone out to me.

I shook my head.

"Sorry, Jenny," Linda said back into it. "Bonnie just left." After she hung up she flopped back onto the sofa. "Jenny sounded jealous because you're here," she reported.

"Did she?" I asked.

"They're all so critical of Ray," Linda went on. "I can't tell them about him living with Les. They would never get over it. Jenny keeps asking me if he's here or not—she's so *suspicious*. She'd love to be the one to tell my mom and dad that he wasn't around. I don't even want to see them. Isn't that great—my own family."

"It's too bad," I said. Then I suggested quietly, "Maybe they could help you."

"They can't," Linda said bluntly. "They don't even know me anymore. And they all hate Ray. They always have. I may not know what to do," she said to the ceiling, "but at least I know what *not* to do."

She looked over at me and added, "Jenny said something about seeing you at school next week." Then she sat up, her face astonished. "Oh my gosh, you'll be going back to *school!*"

I nodded. I'd been putting off the whole subject, wondering how she was going to manage without me. "Next week," I repeated.

"Wow, what a space case. I'd forgotten all about it. What grade are you in?"

"I'm a sophomore." I wanted her to understand that I'd be busier. "It'll be hard to adjust to all the work again," I began.

"Will it?" Linda asked wistfully. "Oh, I always loved it when school started. Everything was new— new teachers, new classes, new clothes. New boyfriends."

"I may not be able to come over as much," I said, more pointedly.

Linda's face fell. She composed it quickly. "Of course you won't," she agreed. "I know what it's like in September. You'll be really busy."

But the brief look had affected me. "I can still stop by sometimes after school," I said.

"Do you think so?" she asked, brightening. "What about watching those detective movies on Saturday nights?"

"I'll still come Saturdays," I said.

She gave me a relieved smile and closed her eyes again.

TEN

In the final week of August I got a postcard from Robert. On the front was a picture of a roadside diner in a small town in Minnesota, with a neon sign in the shape of a piano. On the back of the card were three short sentences: *I tried to write a dozen times. I told you I was a terrible letter writer. Don't kill me when I get back.* It was signed "Roberto," with a huge scrolled R and a long swirl after the O.

I didn't expect to see him until after the weekend, but he came over on Thursday and caught me by surprise. I was coming back from a shopping trip at the mall with my mom, and I had just gotten my hair cut. I gave my packages to my mom and asked her to go ahead inside. We stayed on the porch together. Robert was taller, and he'd gotten his hair cut too. He looked like he had aged two years in a month. We sat down together on the wicker sofa.

"You look different," he said.

"I got a haircut. So did you."

"I got mine from a barber in Minneapolis. He destroyed me."

"No, he didn't, Robert. But you look too old for me now."

He grinned, blushing. "Did you get my card?"

I nodded. "It's a good thing, too. I watched for a letter all month."

"I told you—"

"—you're not much of a letter writer, I know. But I wasn't expecting a letter a day or anything. A paragraph a week would have been fine. I thought you'd forgotten all about me."

"I didn't forget you. I . . . I . . ." He hesitated and looked away. Then he asked, "You don't think this haircut makes me look dumb?"

I looked at him. I was thinking: *This is the first time we've ever sat close together outside of a movie theater.* His arms and legs seemed unbelievably long and tanned. There was a strip of white skin all around the edges of his new haircut. It did look pretty strange up close, but I would never have said so. I had such a good feeling about him being back. "Were you going to say you missed me?" I asked.

He nodded. "I wish we didn't go to different schools," he said sorrowfully.

"It's better this way," I teased. "We won't get tired of each other as fast."

But he looked shocked. "I won't get tired of you, Bonnie," he said. "I mean, I *really* missed you." Then he looked scared for having said it.

"I really missed you too," I said.

He put his arm along the back of the sofa and rested it gingerly against my shoulders. "I've actually never had a girlfriend before," he confessed.

Who would have guessed it? I wondered.

The next night Robert said that he wanted to take me out to dinner, and he suggested a small restaurant close to my house. And he suggested that we walk, which we did, holding hands as though we had always held hands. Because he had been away, he had things to talk about—all I had to do was ask him a few questions and then he told me about Minneapolis and about visiting his grandparents—he had gone fishing with them on their boat. His grandmother had a Chickering piano, and I knew a little about pianos and we talked about our music, about what we hoped to accomplish in the coming year with Mrs. Piccato, whom we both adored. I think a month of missing me had made him more determined to be good company. We talked for over two hours, like old friends. When the check came, Robert told the waitress to give it to me. I looked at him, shocked, and he gave me a crooked smile—he was actually teasing *me*.

"But next time it *will* be my turn to pay," I insisted, recovering.

"Okay, next time," he agreed. "I like the way you're like that."

"Like what?"

"The way you just come right out and say what you want," he explained. "My mom would like you too."

We walked home the long way, holding hands again. When we got close to my house, I asked him if he felt like coming inside to see my parents. "They haven't seen you since July," I reminded him. "And you don't have to be nervous. They really like you."

"I can't *decide* not to be nervous," he said. "I'm a nervous person."

"I mean you don't have to worry about making a good impression. You can just be yourself."

"Being myself means being nervous." But he laughed at himself.

"Okay, then, be nervous!" I giggled.

"I'm more relaxed when I can be nervous," he said, and we both laughed harder. We were in front of my house and I tried to stop giggling. "Well, do you want to come in?" I asked.

"Next time," he promised. "When I'm feeling more like myself—nervous."

We broke up again and then stopped in the same moment. And very quickly, me stretching up, him stretching down, we kissed. It was so natural. We didn't bump heads or lock braces or any of the things that had happened to me before—it was a graceful kiss. It ended with us smiling at each other.

I was sorry I couldn't tell Linda about that first kiss. She of course assumed I had been kissing Robert all summer. But I could tell her that things were more serious, that we were really boyfriend and girlfriend now. She gave me a hug, happy for me, and then wondered aloud again if my Robert was anything like her Howie.

"He was so sweet, and I never really appreciated him." She sighed. "He just wasn't the one, know what I mean? And I wanted to be swept away. I wanted things to be crazy and fast and wild. Lou knew what I meant. She went out with him a few times too. God, we used to share everything."

Then she went into a long story about a time

when she and Lou had both dated Howie in the same weekend and they'd spent all day Sunday comparing every little detail. "Those were the days," she finished softly.

Something inside me snapped. "Don't say that," I said.

"Don't say what?"

"Don't start that those-were-the-days stuff. Like you're already old or something."

Linda's face fell. "Already old?"

"It's just that sometimes you make it sound like your whole life is over."

"Do I?" Linda asked. She seemed about to cry. "Jesus, Ray says that, too."

But the thought of *him* saying this enraged me. "Oh, *he* probably just thinks you should go out and drink every weekend like he does," I blurted.

It was the first time I had ever openly criticized Ray. Linda looked all the more stricken. "Don't get the wrong idea about Ray," she objected softly. "He's doing the best he can. He really is."

So I asked, "Then why hasn't he come back yet?"

Linda hesitated, but answered calmly, "He's been spending a lot of time on Les' boat, getting himself together. He'll be home in a few weeks."

But it had already been several weeks, and I couldn't hide my skepticism. Linda caught it. She went on, mechanically, I thought. "Things will work out between me and Ray. All couples go through rough times. He's doing the best he can. . . ."

Jeremy came crawling into the room, and I lifted him up and walked away with him, not wanting to hear any more.

". . . You'll understand better," Linda finished mournfully, "when you're married."

ELEVEN

Now I had to tell Robert that I had agreed to still spend Saturday nights at Linda's. I expected him to understand.

"Every Saturday?" he asked, before I could explain. "Couldn't they find another baby-sitter sometimes?"

"Well, it's not just baby-sitting anymore," I explained. "It's more than that. The thing is . . . while you were away, things sort of . . . went downhill between Linda and Ray. He isn't even there anymore, actually. He's living with a friend."

"You mean they're *separated*?" Robert asked, grimacing.

I nodded.

"Are they going to get a *divorce*?"

"I don't know. Linda says it's temporary."

"Well, where does she go when you baby-sit?"

"Actually, she doesn't go anywhere. We both stay home with Jeremy. I'm trying to help her."

Robert still looked confused. "Why do you have to help her?" he asked. "Doesn't she have any friends? What about her family?"

"Linda used to have friends," I said. "She was one of the most popular girls at St. Martins. But they've all gone away to college. And her relationship with her family isn't that great."

"Well, I can see why," Robert interjected. "After what she put them through last year."

Now I was quiet. It surprised me—the cold tone in Robert's voice. I'd been on the verge of asking him to come with me sometime to Linda's, but his attitude made me hesitate. Finally, he said, more thoughtfully, "You should be careful not to get caught in the middle of something."

Robert's face had grown so long and unhappy that I impulsively put an arm around him. I could feel his shoulders sagging even through the thickness of his parka.

"What's the matter?" I asked him.

He shook his head and rearranged his expression. "Oh nothing," he said. "I just thought of something sad."

*   *   *

The next Friday St. Martins played against Central, and Robert and I went to the game together. It was the first really public thing we had ever done together, and we were both excited. At halftime he introduced me to some of his friends, and I introduced him to mine. I felt really happy in the bleachers beside him.

Then I looked up over my shoulder and saw Jenny Mason above me near the top of the stands. She saw me in the same moment and waved. She was with her new friends, but she gestured to me to come up. I waved back at her, but pretended not to understand that she was beckoning to me and turned around again.

Robert had looked too. "Who is that?" he asked me. "Does she want you to go up there?"

"Don't turn around again," I instructed him. "It's Jenny Mason."

"I think she wants to talk to you. Don't you speak to her at all?"

"Not tonight," I insisted quietly. "She'll want to talk about her sister."

"How do you know?"

"I just know."

Robert was watching me closely. "Didn't you tell me that Jenny Mason used to be your best friend?" he asked.

"But I don't want to talk about Linda tonight," I explained pleadingly. "I just want to be with you."

I thought he would be happy to hear me say this. But he looked troubled. Then he turned slowly and glanced once more at Jenny.

On the walk home, he brought it up again. "Bonnie," he wondered, "why do you think Jenny Mason wanted to ask you about her own sister?"

"I told you before," I explained, "Linda doesn't confide in her family. She says it's because they never liked Ray in the first place. Although lately I've been feeling like they're probably right about him. Linda seems to think things will change, but I can't see how—"

"Maybe things *will* change," Robert interrupted quietly.

I shook my head. "*He* won't change."

"Do you know him?" Robert asked. "Have you ever talked to him?"

"No, but from everything I've seen—"

"But if you don't know him, how can you be so sure?"

I glared at him and was surprised to see him glaring back. Robert looked away first. "Don't you think," he said for the second time, "that it's better

111

not to get caught in the middle of something like this?"

"I *am* in the middle," I said. "Linda is my friend. I think you'll understand why I feel this way once you've met her and seen for yourself how—"

"I don't think I want to meet her," Robert protested.

"Robert! She's been asking me to bring you over since you went to visit your mom. She's really dying to meet you."

"I hate meeting people who've been dying to meet me," he pleaded. "I get nervous and end up making a bad impression."

"Robert—"

"Let's just enjoy the walk home, okay? We'll talk about it when we get to your house."

But he didn't bring it up again.

On Monday I had just sat down in the cafeteria when I looked up and found Jenny standing across from me with her tray.

"Can I sit with you?" she asked.

I nodded, and she sat down.

"I was sorry we don't have any classes together this fall," she said hesitantly. "I never see you anymore."

I shrugged evasively. "I've been pretty busy."

"Was that your boyfriend I saw you with at the

game? He looked really nice. When did you meet him?"

"In the summer. He goes to Central."

"I met a guy this summer, too, but we broke up in August." Then she waited to see if I would say something sympathetic.

"That's too bad," I said, wondering what would come next.

"I was surprised when you answered the telephone at my sister's," Jenny said.

"She needed a baby-sitter," I said, wanting to play it down.

"She never asked *me*," Jenny complained.

"Come on, Jenny. You know why she didn't."

"Oh, I suppose," she admitted. "But I *would* have. So how long have you been baby-sitting for her?"

"I started in the summer." Then I added, "After we stopped hanging around together."

Jenny nodded, acknowledging my point. We ate silently for a few moments. "Bonnie," she began again, "do you think my sister is doing okay?"

I hesitated. "Well, I'm only her baby-sitter."

"She never comes home now, no matter what we plan. And whenever I call her, day or night, Ray is never there. She says he's working overtime, but that doesn't sound like Ray. Does she ever say anything to you about it?"

I shook my head.

"Is he ever home when you're there?"

I shook my head again.

"I've been wondering if things are going okay for them."

I hesitated one last minute and then blurted, "Ray is living with some other guy on a boat!" It was such a relief to tell someone.

Jenny put down her sandwich. "You're kidding! Is Linda alone with Jeremy all the time?"

"Except when I'm there."

"What does she do all day?"

"I don't think she does anything. She sits around thinking about her old high-school days. Or else sleeping. She sleeps a lot."

"She must be awfully depressed. Has she ever mentioned moving back home? My parents would say yes. I heard them talking about it."

"I don't think she wants to do that," I said.

"Well, has she said anything about getting a divorce?"

"Oh no. And if I say anything against Ray, she defends him. She says things like 'all couples have their problems.'"

"At least she talks to you. She would never have told me. I'm worried about her, Bonnie."

Then I felt suspicious, remembering our fights.

"Why *now*, Jenny?" I asked. "You weren't worried in the least a year ago."

"Neither were you," she accused back. "You thought it was the coolest thing anybody had ever done."

We drew back from each other, an old standoff. Then I said, "You're right." I smiled ruefully.

Her expression softened too. "Now when I think of her in that crummy little apartment and all her friends gone—you had to have known her before, Bonnie. She was always in the center of things. She had so many friends. And all these boyfriends . . ."

"I do remember," I said. "I thought she was like a movie star."

"Remember how I used to complain about boys calling her all the time? The phone ringing night and day?"

We were both silent a moment with our own memories of Linda. Then Jenny said firmly, "You have to talk to her, Bonnie. Tell her not to waste any more of her life on Ray Pastrovitch."

"I can't tell her that!" I protested.

"Why not? She'd listen to you."

"I don't know enough about things like that," I insisted. "I can't give marriage advice!"

"Then who will?"

"I don't know," I said. The bell rang, rescuing me. "I have to go," I mumbled, standing up.

"Will you at least think about it?" she asked. And I said yes, knowing I would be doing that anyway.

Mondays we had our piano lessons, and afterward Robert and I liked to walk to a special drugstore downtown with an old-fashioned fountain. I was particularly eager to sit down with him in a quiet place, hoping to bring up the touchy subject of Linda again. Jenny's words had made me feel more than ever like I needed someone to help me figure out the right thing to do.

Our favorite booth was at the farthest corner of the drugstore, and I hurried back, anxious to talk. But there, in the last booth, sat Ray Pastrovitch, and beside him was a red-haired woman, as tall as he was, with one long arm around his neck. She was whispering something into his ear, and he was laughing. I turned on the heels of my shoes so fast that my rubber soles screeched, and left poor Robert in the medicine aisle behind me. He came out of the store a few moments later, wearing a bewildered expression, craning his long neck to find me. I waved to him from behind a parked car.

"What are you doing over there?" he called, exasperated.

I waved him closer. When he reached the car, I grabbed his arm and began walking again, hurrying him down the block, away from the drugstore.

"What is your hurry?" he asked me. "I thought you wanted to sit down."

"Linda's husband was sitting in the back booth," I said breathlessly. *"Ray."*

"What are you whispering for? Is there something wrong with a person being in a drugstore?"

"He was with another *woman*," I said. "They were scrunched up together in the last booth. If he'd seen me, I would have died."

"Maybe it was just somebody he works with," Robert said practically.

"She was hanging all *over* him. God. Right out in public, not caring who saw them." I was clenching my fists.

Robert was silent, walking beside me. "Maybe this is something his wife already knows about," he suggested quietly.

I stopped in my tracks. "Robert! She *doesn't*. She thinks he spends all his time with an old friend."

"Well, maybe that was his sister or his cousin or someone like that."

"Why are you defending him?" I exclaimed. "We saw him with our own eyes, right there in the—"

"You saw him," he corrected me. "But you don't know what he was doing there. And you don't know anything about him—you admitted that before."

We had both stopped walking, and we stood facing each other. "Why are you defending him?" I asked again.

Robert scowled. "You were beginning to sound like my mother. When she uses her all-men-are-bastards voice."

I was stunned. In the silence we began slowly to walk again. Finally I said, "Robert, I never said I think all men are bastards."

"I know you didn't," he said. "I shouldn't have said that. It's just that this subject makes me so uncomfortable. I don't like to think of you in the middle. It can get really bad."

"But I'm already in the middle. And I was hoping you would help me."

"I don't think there's anything either of us can do to help," he said.

"Are you saying no? That you won't help me?"

He sighed unhappily. "What are you asking me

to do exactly? Do you want me to go over there with you sometime?"

"Oh, Robert, once you do, I think you'll understand why I want to help Linda. Why she's important to me. Please?"

He looked caught and miserable. But he was too nice to say no. He rolled his eyes worriedly and promised he'd come to Linda's the next Saturday.

TWELVE

But when we climbed the steps to Linda's door, when I saw through Robert's eyes how run-down the outside of the house was and noticed the torn garbage bags piled on the landing and saw how the screen door was held into the rotting frame with tape, I knew I had made a mistake. Robert was silent, and I could feel him taking in the bleakness, judging it. I had a brief moment of hope when Linda threw open the door—she looked thrilled to see me; her face was flushed and her smile was dazzling.

"Come in!" she cried. "At last I get to meet the mystery man." But there was something about her voice—it was unusually shrill, almost frantic. Something was wrong. She pulled us both into her kitchen, laughing a laugh that wasn't real. She was upset, covering something up. I sat between Robert and Linda at the table, feeling the awful weight of my mistake.

I tried to catch her eye, wanting her to calm down, but she was chattering and laughing at her own jokes and waving her arms without really looking at either of us. Every few minutes she would lift Jeremy from the floor, press him against her, and call him her poor darling, her poor angel, while he whined and squirmed the whole time. *What's wrong with you?* I asked her silently. *What's the matter?*

Robert listened politely, his back arched with nervousness. He was as tongue-tied as he'd warned me he'd be, although Linda was talking enough for all three of us, going on about her wonderful high-school days, stories that I had already heard. I looked around the kitchen. On the hook beside the door I noticed Ray's blue windbreaker; I hadn't seen it there in weeks. There was an empty beer can on the sink. Then I excused myself and went into the bathroom, despite Robert's look of alarm that I would leave him alone with Linda.

Beside the bathroom sink a towel was striped with grease from Ray's garage, and his work jeans were hanging on the back of the door. Suddenly it seemed that the whole apartment was full of Ray, like he would pop out any moment. When

I came out of the bathroom, Linda was still chattering, telling Robert a story about Lou. Jeremy was trying to crawl up into Robert's lap, leaving fingerprints up and down his pant leg. Robert flashed a please-help-me look.

"We have to be going, Linda," I announced. "We both have tons of homework."

Linda seemed both relieved and disappointed. "Homework," she said. "Right. God, lately I wish I'd done a little more of it."

She lifted the squirming Jeremy to one hip and walked out on the landing, waving down at us, lifting Jeremy's arm, making him wave, too.

"Come back, Robert," she called. "Anytime."

When we reached the corner, Robert sighed with relief. I felt a sharp pang of protectiveness toward Linda.

"Didn't I tell you she was wonderful?" I barked at him.

"Yes," he said quietly. He paused, thinking. "But I think something was wrong with her."

"What do you mean—wrong?"

"I think she was upset. Trying to hide it. Talking nonstop like that. It made me kind of uncomfortable."

"You're always uncomfortable," I snapped.

Robert was thinking, figuring it out. "Maybe it's because I know too many things about her.

Personal things. I know she's in this depressing situation, but she was trying very hard to act like this really happy person. And the way she went on and on about being in high school, like she'd give anything to do it again. I can't believe anyone would—"

"Could we just drop it please? You obviously don't understand."

Robert looked hurt. He said, "Bonnie, I'm trying to explain why I felt uncomfortable up there."

"I don't want to talk about it, okay?"

"All right," he said coldly. "But I don't want to go there ever again. So don't ask me to."

We fell into step together, both upset. I had really wanted Robert to be drawn to Linda, to feel like she was important. But I knew I'd made a mistake thinking he would see in her what I had seen when I'd first met her. She just wasn't the same person anymore. Ray had destroyed her.

I called Linda's name at the door and let myself back in. "I'm back," I called. "It's just me this time, by myself."

In the living room I saw that Jeremy had fallen asleep at one end of the couch with his blanket and his bottle. *You didn't even put him to bed,* I thought.

"Make yourself at home!" Linda called from the

bedroom. "I was just resting, I'll be right out."

Linda came out of the bedroom in her bathrobe, smiling, her eyes red. She watched me pick Jeremy up and carry him, past her, into the bedroom. I laid him in his crib and covered him up. Linda stood in the bedroom doorway, watching me. When she spoke, it was with the same forced cheeriness.

"Oh, honey, I'm glad you came back. I really wanted to talk to you. It was neat to meet your boyfriend. God, he's so tall! And somehow I expected him to look younger. He's even taller than Ray! I see what you mean about him being quiet. But there's something very intense about him. He's a thinker, isn't he? The intellectual type. I would have probably guessed that he's a musician. He's a perfect—"

"Linda," I interrupted, "was Ray here today?"

She pulled her bathrobe more tightly around her. "How did you know?" she asked.

I shrugged. "I saw his jacket. Did you guys talk or anything?"

"Did I seem upset? Could you tell? Did your boyfriend—"

"He couldn't tell. But I noticed because I . . . know you better."

She nodded and sat down, laying her head against the back of the sofa. "He walked in the door, and

Bonnie, I just got all these old feelings back. You know what I mean?"

"Is he coming back?" I asked.

Linda lifted her chin. "Oh, he'll be back," she insisted. "He still loves me, Bonnie."

"*When* will he be back?"

"Where did your boyfriend go?" she asked. "What do you call him? Robert instead of Bob? That's so sweet."

"Linda, when is Ray coming back?"

"Ray and I used to meet each other after school every day. We always felt like we'd been apart for weeks. If we didn't see each other every day, we'd go crazy. Oh, Bonnie," she said softly, "do you ever feel like you'll just die if you can't be with him every single minute?"

"No," I said.

She looked at me. "But you really like Robert, don't you?"

"I like him," I said. "But I don't feel like I'll *die* when he isn't around."

She leaned close to me. "Tell me something," she said. "Do you guys . . . have you ever—"

"No," I said quickly.

"Not even once? But haven't the two of you at least—"

"No!"

"But what will you do when—"

"Linda!" I cried. "It just isn't like that for us! Robert is my first real boyfriend, *ever*."

We looked at each other. Linda drew back and covered her face.

"I'm a lot younger than you are," I said. It was the first time I'd wanted to admit it.

"It isn't that," she said from behind her hands. "It isn't our ages."

What is it, then? I pleaded silently, but Linda said she was tired. She went back into the bedroom and I went home.

THIRTEEN

I avoided Jenny during the school day, and afterward I left the building through a different exit, avoiding the spot where I often met Robert. Because I couldn't face either of them.

And for the first time since I'd met her, I didn't want to go to Linda's apartment. Jenny was wrong—I couldn't help Linda. Not alone.

A week passed this way. The weather was overcast and chilly, and this made me feel even more like hiding. On Monday I even called Mrs. Piccato to cancel my piano lesson. "I have too much homework," I explained guiltily.

"Don't worry, Bonita, I know how things get this time of the semester," Mrs. Piccato said soothingly. "Roberto told me the same thing."

I hung up the phone, sick at the possibility that

Robert didn't want to face me either. *Maybe he's been avoiding me at the same time I've been avoiding him,* I thought. It was unbearable. My Robert.

I dialed the phone again. "It's me," I said when he answered. "I think we need to talk."

"I know," he agreed. He sounded very relieved. "I know I should have called you but . . . but . . ."

"It's okay," I said softly.

"No, it's not okay. I'm sorry I've been avoiding you. I've been feeling terrible about it, but I needed some time to think things through."

"So did I."

"Bonnie, we keep having the same fights about the same thing. Those people. And I'm starting to get the feeling that you don't really listen to me when I try to tell you how I feel. Lately it feels like you're dragging me into some things that I just don't think I can handle."

"But Linda isn't just *some things*!"

"I know you think she's your friend, but Bonnie, she's much older than we are, and I think she's made some pretty big mistakes in her life. Did you ever consider that she likes having you around because she knows she can get you to do things for her?"

"It isn't like that!" I said, shocked. "You don't understand—she really *is* my friend!" I was on the verge of tears. My head was spinning. The same feeling I'd had with Linda last week—that things were too different between us—now I was feeling it with Robert.

"Bonnie?" he asked. "Bonnie, are you still there?"

"I'm here," I said numbly. "I don't want to talk about this anymore. It's too confusing."

Now Robert was silent. Then his voice sounded once again gentle and relieved. "I missed you like crazy all week," he said. "Did you miss me?"

"Yes," I wailed. Then I hung up and burst into tears.

When I ate my lunch for the first time in a week in the cafeteria, Jenny quickly found me. She slammed her books on the table dramatically.

"Where have you been for the past week?" she cried. "I looked for you every day!"

"Did you?" I asked, bracing myself.

"Bonnie, I found out where Ray is spending all his time, and it isn't with his old high-school pal, or whatever Linda has been telling you."

She sat down beside me on the cafeteria bench and put her head close to mine. "He's not with his friends at all, the bastard. He has a new *girlfriend*. A friend of mine lives on Slayton near the bluff," Jenny went on, "right across the street from where this new girlfriend lives. She says Ray Pastrovitch's car is over there all hours of the day *and* night. I even saw him myself, leaving her apartment on a Saturday *morning*."

"Does she have red hair?" I asked.

Jenny looked at me, surprised. "How did you know?" she asked.

I sighed. "I saw them too, Jenny. Downtown."

Jenny shook her head in disbelief. "Right downtown?" she asked. "In broad daylight? Oh, god, Linda must be devastated."

"I don't think she knows," I said. "She still says that Ray is living on a boat with a guy named Les."

"Oh, come on, Bonnie—how can Linda *not* know?" Jenny cried. "Everybody in town must know!"

"She doesn't want to know, Jenny."

"Oh, Bonnie, somebody has to make her see that—"

"Don't start in on me again," I protested. "I tried to say something last week, and she went off on this thing about how it was with her and Ray in the beginning, how much they couldn't stand to be apart and everything. I never know what to say when she starts that. Then she asks me if I feel that way about Robert."

"Do you?" Jenny asked.

I turned the question around. "Did you? With the guy you met last summer?"

"I asked you first."

I sighed. "I like him a lot. But I've been feeling lately like he doesn't understand me."

Jenny nodded. "It was the same with me and Paul. I liked him, but I was never sure if I really knew him. Sometimes he seemed like a complete stranger. I never really got very close to him."

"I wonder what it would be like," I said wistfully, "to be so completely in love with somebody."

"I know. Crazy in love."

"Like they were."

Jenny put her chin in her hands. "Yeah, but look where it got *them*."

"Do you think you can feel that way about someone," I wondered aloud, "and not end up in a mess?"

"I don't know."

We were both silent a moment. Then Jenny looked at me intently. "Bonnie," she said, "who is going to tell Linda what Ray is doing if you won't?"

"How about you?" I insisted. "You're her *sister*!"

"Come on—you know she'll never listen to me. I've never been able to say anything about Ray."

"But it will sound so terrible! How can I even

say the words? 'Oh, by the way, your husband has a new girlfriend.' I can't do it, Jenny!"

"Bonnie, you're the only friend she has. And Ray is making a complete fool of her!"

I was backing away and Jenny grabbed my hand. "Please, Bonnie. I don't want to see Linda get any worse."

A certain resolve came over me. "Neither do I," I said softly.

"Then you'll tell her?"

"I don't know how," I said. "But I will."

FOURTEEN

I still can't say exactly why I decided to drag Robert in one more time. He had asked me out on a Saturday night without any mention of Linda. He was testing me. And so I turned it around, testing him.

"Why are we going this way?" Robert asked, when I steered him down Slayton Street in the dark.

"For a change," I said. He must have thought I just wanted our walk to take a little longer, and he smiled and put his arm around me, hugging my shoulders tight.

I hugged his waist, too, but stiffly—I was scanning the curbs and driveways in the dark, looking for Ray's car. Then I saw it, parked in a lot near the doorway to an apartment complex across the street. I caught my breath and managed to steer Robert closer, so that he would see it too. I was rehearsing a way to nonchalantly point it out, since it hadn't been terribly visible from across the street.

"Now where are we going?" Robert wondered.

"It's not as dark on this side," I said, which was true. There was a streetlight right above the parking lot I was moving toward. But as we reached the edge of the lot, to my dismay Ray Pastrovitch himself and the red-haired woman came out of the apartment building, only a few yards from where Robert and I were walking. There was no time to escape. And Ray saw me the same moment that I saw him. The woman had one of her arms wrapped around Ray; she was still laughing at something he had said before he saw me. But Ray's face darkened as he recognized me.

"It's Ray," I whispered. I stopped in my tracks. Robert tightened his grip around my shoulder.

"Is that Bonnie?" Ray called out to me. "What are *you* doing here?"

"I live close by," I managed to say. I pointed up the street. Ray glanced toward where I was pointing and then back at me. His eyes narrowed.

"Funny, I thought you might be spying on me."

For an instant I couldn't reply.

"You weren't *spying* on me, were you?" he asked.

"*God*, Ray!" the woman scolded.

I found my voice. "I have a lot better things to do," I began furiously, "than—"

"We were just coming home from the movies," Robert interrupted, squeezing my shoulders. "We're a little late getting home."

Then Ray looked at Robert and his expression changed. He looked like he realized he'd made a mistake. "Oh, right," he said, trying to sound more conversational. "What's playing?"

"We saw the new Spielberg," Robert said. His voice was surprisingly calm. "It was pretty good." Then he pulled my arm gently, directing us past them. "Got to get going," he said. He started walking faster.

"Who was that?" I heard the woman ask Ray, behind us.

Ray answered, "Jeremy's baby-sitter."

When we were safely on the next block, I exploded, "Did you hear what he said? Did you hear how he accused me of—"

"Is that why we were walking this way?"

"How could he dare to stand there like that and say—"

"Is that why we were *walking* this way?"

I reacted pleadingly to the anger in Robert's voice. "That woman he was with," I cried, "he lives with her now. Linda doesn't know. She thinks he's living with a *friend*!"

Robert didn't answer. He was looking away.

"Linda doesn't know," I repeated frantically. "Jenny thinks I should tell her. She has no one but me to help her."

Finally he looked at me. "Didn't you listen to a single thing I said to you last week?" he asked.

"Yes! Of course I listened. But can't you see why I have to do something about this?"

There was a terrible silence. When Robert finally spoke, his voice was cold, colder than I had ever heard it. "I've tried to explain how I feel. If you want to live in this soap opera, go ahead. I can't take it anymore. I'm going home."

He began walking away. If he had looked back at me, he would have seen my tears. He walked straight to the end of the block and then turned out of sight without ever looking back.

"I can't take it anymore either," I whispered. I went home to get my bike and then headed back to Baker Street.

I hadn't seen her in almost two weeks—the longest I had been away since that first night in June, so long ago. She opened the door wearing her faded bathrobe.

"Thought it might be you. Saturday night, right?" She smiled ironically.

"Were you asleep?" I asked.

"Oh no," she said, shrugging, looking down at her wrinkled robe. "No, I just didn't bother to—" She stopped and looked more closely at my face. "Hey, are you crying?" she asked softly. "Why are you crying, Bonnie?"

"Because of *you*," I said. "Because I don't know how to help you."

"Help me?"

"I don't see how you can keep on like this, not doing anything, not going out. It's not good for you. I wish I could help you, but I don't know what to do anymore."

She was still looking at me, surprised. Finally she leaned into the doorframe, lowered her eyes, and shook her head. Then she asked quietly, "Do you want to come in, Bonnie?"

But I stood in the door, unwilling to come inside until I had said everything. "I don't know how to say this, but I think you should just admit that . . . admit that . . ."

"That Ray isn't coming back?" she asked.

"That Ray isn't coming back," I echoed. We stared at each other.

"Hey, come on in," she said. "Here. Sit down." She pulled a chair away from the table for me.

"Linda, I'm sorry I haven't been over," I said, sitting down. "I hated seeing you this way."

"God, have I been that bad?"

I nodded. She nodded too, agreeing with me.

"Well, I had to be sure, you know," she insisted tiredly. "For Jeremy's sake, I had to be. I couldn't give up on him overnight. It was a marriage, after all, crazy or not."

"Are you sure now?"

Linda hesitated an instant and then said, "Bonnie, I honestly think he must be seeing another woman."

"I know," I agreed softly. But Linda's eyes widened.

"What do you mean, you *know*?"

"I've seen them," I said. "So has Jenny. He's living with another woman."

Her mouth fell open. She looked like I had punched her. Then she stood up and leaned for support against the kitchen wall. She closed her eyes. I stood up in alarm.

"I'm all right," she whispered. "Part of me expected you to say, 'Don't be silly, Ray would never do that.' My last shred of hope and all that. There it goes." Then she lowered herself slowly to the floor, sat on the dirty linoleum and started to cry. It was a different kind of crying, though. It wasn't wistful or confused. It sounded final. I sat down on the floor beside her and put my arms around her.

"Oh, it was so beautiful when it all started," she cried.

"I know," I said. And then, realizing all I didn't know, I added sadly, "I wish I understood."

I gave her a Kleenex and she wiped her tears. We both sat together a little longer, and then Linda pulled herself away, struggling to stand up. "No more sitting around crying," she said. "I don't want you to see me like this anymore. Sit down and I'll make us something hot to drink."

"Okay," I said.

She made hot chocolate and we sat sipping it, both slightly dazed. A calm had settled over the tiny apartment. I could hear Jeremy's breathing from the bedroom.

"Is he all right?" I asked.

"Yeah, he's fine," she said. "He's a great little kid. I've been wishing he could talk so he could tell me what I should do next." She laughed softly.

"In a few more months he probably will," I said, laughing too.

"You've been such a friend to me, Bonnie," Linda said. "Man, I've really dumped a lot of stuff on you."

"It's all right," I said.

"I think I wanted you to figure all of this out with me. Together with me. The way Lou used

139

to." Linda sighed. "We always shared our problems. Even before we had any."

"Why don't you write to her and tell her what's happened?" I suggested. "Tell her about Ray leaving and everything."

"Oh, I've tried to stay in touch with her," Linda said. "I don't know. I think she's changed."

"Well, so have you," I reminded her. "She probably thinks everything with you and Ray is just fine. Maybe she thinks you don't need her. Maybe it would be different if she knew what's happened."

"Maybe," Linda echoed.

"It's what I would do," I said.

Linda covered her face with her hands. "What if she says 'I told you so'?" she groaned. "Or what if she just doesn't care?"

"But wasn't she your best friend?" I asked.

Linda uncovered her face. "Yes. She was."

"For years and years?"

Linda nodded. She said softly, "Maybe you're right. Why not? It's worth another try. I'll just tell her the truth."

When I got up to leave, she put her arms around me and hugged me. She had grown so thin, it was like hugging a child. I was filled with hope that when she wrote to Lou, Lou would be a friend, and wouldn't say I told you so or that she didn't care. I hoped that they would become friends again. Because I knew better than anyone how much Linda needed someone to be more than just a story from the old days.

When I walked from the bottom of the stairs to my bicycle, I saw a shadow move along the side of the house. It startled me. I half expected to see Ray, his face accusing and angry because of what I had said to Linda. But the small yard was silent. I quickly jumped on my bike and rode home. There was no need to dread Ray's coming home anymore. Even Linda had admitted he was gone.

Dear Lou,

I know I said I wouldn't write to you again, but I was wrong. I've been wrong about a lot of things this year. You've known me longer than anybody, Lou, so you're the one I'm turning to. If you don't care anymore, then don't answer this letter, and I'll know what your silence means.

Ray left me, Lou. He's really gone. I've been making excuses for him, telling people he's still around, but tonight I faced the truth and I know it's over. And as soon as I faced it and let go of all my dreams, who should knock at my door but Ray himself, coming to finally tell me he's not coming back. He started crying— I'd never seen him crying before, Lou. And so I made

143

it easy for him. I asked him if he'd come to say good-bye, and he shook his head yes. Then I asked him if there was somebody else, and he shook his head yes again. And the strange thing is that I had just spent half the night crying my eyes out with Jeremy's baby-sitter, so hearing him say it didn't even faze me. I felt like I'd already heard it a million times. I felt like the whole thing had happened too long ago to hurt any-more. I didn't even feel jealous. Because I know that he couldn't help it. He's just a big kid, Lou, disguised as a man. He's really about twelve years old. I felt like I was talking with my little brother. My big, sorry, overgrown little brother. I didn't hate him. I even made coffee for him. All the things you said about him are true, but I don't hate him.

Tonight I beg you, on every day of every year of our friendship, not to ever ever say I told you so about Ray.

Last night, before he came over, I sat on the floor crying with Jeremy's baby-sitter, and she said she wished she understood what it was like when it all started. And I just couldn't find the words, Lou. I couldn't describe the me who did all those crazy things. I looked backward inside myself, and it was like looking for a person who is so long gone that you can't even remem-ber her face anymore. All I could picture was this one night on the beach on the Gulf, inside Ray's sleeping *bag, looking up at the sky and listening to Ray breathing and feeling all happy because I knew that the next night we were going to make love again in some other place and I would look up at the same sky and hear the same beautiful silence after he fell asleep. When I remembered that, I thought,* That was me, that's what it was all about, that whole trip. *But how could I tell this kid about* that? *She's so young and innocent—I don't think she's ever even* wanted *to have sex. Last night I envied her. She's so smart and so naive at the same time. It makes me feel* old, *Lou. And I'm nineteen. So all I did was sit on the floor and cry. And this young, sweet kid put her arms around me and comforted me. And she didn't even know why I was crying. She didn't know what I was saying good-bye to. I couldn't have explained it in a million years.*

Well, I have to get my life together now. I've been living like a zombie for the past few months—refusing to see what was right in front of my nose. I have to pull myself out of it for Jeremy. You know that old cliché—no place to go but up. Next week I'm going to look for a job. And I'm going to go back to high school—I was a complete idiot not to do that the minute I got back to town. I still have a little money in the bank that nobody knows about. And Ray says he knows this guy who does divorces really cheap.

If you have any advice for me, I'm all ears. But right now, I'm so tired I can hardly see straight. I'm going to bed. I hope you will answer me. I need you, old friend, more than ever.

Love,
Linda

FIFTEEN

The next morning Robert came to my house. I heard him talking to my mom and dad, and I came out of my upstairs room and watched him a moment from the stairs. He was making a special effort to converse with my parents, which I knew was hard for him. I remembered how he had quietly stood up to Ray the night before, staying calm for my sake. I realized that there was a peculiar bravery to him—from our first date he had displayed it. He was always pushing himself, forcing himself in his shy way to handle difficult things. When he turned and saw me on the steps, he didn't smile: His face was a question. I smiled.

"I'm surprised you came," I said, as we began

walking away from the house. It was a cold clear day. Leaves were blowing in circles around us as we walked. "I thought you'd stay mad a long time, maybe forever."

"I just wish it hadn't happened," Robert said sadly. "It makes me feel like you don't know me."

"Sometimes I feel like that too," I reminded him.

He took a deep breath. "But I've thought it over, Bonnie. I don't want to stop being with you because of what happened."

"Me either."

"I want to keep trying to understand you. You're the closest friend I've ever had." He took my hand and squeezed it.

"I don't want you to think I don't listen to you, Robert," I said, leaning into his shoulder. "I do listen, and I'll try even harder."

He looked down at me. His eyes were bright. "I want to tell you some things," he said, "about when my mom and dad split up. And I was caught in the middle."

"Okay," I said.

He took a deep breath. "But not now. I just want to be with you for a little while."

"Me too. What should we do?"

"Would you want to go for a bike ride?" he asked. "We won't have too many more this year. Or do you think it's too cold?"

"It's not too cold."

He put my hand into his pocket with his. And we walked back to my house to get our bikes.

SIXTEEN

I saw Linda a few more times before she left. She was packing hurriedly, totally engrossed in what she was about to do. Sometimes she would come across something that would make her sad, like Ray's ragged sleeping bag or a stray photograph of the two of them, but she would brush her tears away impatiently.

It seemed to help her to have me around watching her pack. She didn't talk to me, though, in the ways I'd grown used to, the stories, the memories.

She tossed her old dishes into a garbage bag. "Out they go," she said. "Lou says she already has dishes. And the less stuff I haul with me, the better, don't you think?"

When I didn't answer, she stopped and looked

over at me. I looked away. She was so eager to leave. I felt that along with the dishes, she was throwing me away too.

She put the bag down and came closer. "We wish we could take Bonnie with us, don't we, Jeremy?" she said. And to me, "It all would have been so much worse, Bonnie, if not for you."

I nodded, acknowledging everything. Jeremy wrapped his arms around my knees. My eyes filled with tears as I picked him up, and Linda and I smiled at each other over his head. She went back to her cupboards.

So I kept Jeremy out of her way as best I could. It was my last chance to spend time with her. My last chance with Jeremy, too, and I knew I'd miss him terribly. I was glad he was a baby. He didn't know.

When it had been months since I'd seen Ray, I asked Jenny what became of him.

"I'm not sure, but I think he moved to Kalamazoo with that woman," she said.

"Do you think he ever sees Jeremy?" I wondered.

"I don't think so. But they say it's easier this way—with Jeremy still a baby."

"Do they really say that?"

She nodded. "I hope it's true."

Jenny had been upset by Linda's decision to move in with Lou in Oregon instead of coming home. She had no idea that I had been partly responsible for it. She was still grateful that I had told Linda what was really going on. "It's not your fault," she had said, "that Linda decided to run away *again*."

That was the way she saw it. I disagreed, of course, but it didn't prevent us from becoming friends again.

But there were unanswered questions from that summer. I felt a tug when I rode past the Baker Street house and saw that a different young couple lived upstairs. Now I was almost the same age Linda had been when she'd met Ray, and I was as mystified as ever. Sometimes I felt dissatisfied and unsettled, like I had too much still to learn and too many changes ahead to muddle through.

I was closer than before to Robert, but there was something different between us too. There was a way in which we could not blend, would not agree. I still couldn't explain why the whole idea of Linda breaking away from St. Martins had been so important to me in the first place. He didn't understand why people did such things. He would probably always see Linda as someone who I was lucky to be done with. Like Jenny, he thought she had run away again, this time even farther than before. He believed in his heart that she had done one of the worst things in the world—treated a marriage like a mere passing phase. However much his parents had hurt him, they had at least never done that.

I was walking along the bluff with him in the spring, my mind full of things Linda had said at her kitchen table, late at night. I remembered she'd said that she and Ray couldn't stand to be apart. I was wondering for the hundredth time what it would be like to feel that way about someone. What if I never felt for myself what Linda had felt toward Ray? And could a person feel those things without completely losing herself, as Linda had done? And if I never felt that way, would I grow up regretting it? What if nothing in my life ever really pulled me away from what was safe and comfortable?

"What are you thinking about?" Robert asked.

I hesitated—it made him uncomfortable if I brought up Linda. So it was Jenny I mentioned. "I was just thinking about something Jenny said. She asked me if I could ever imagine myself running away."

"Us running away?" Robert protested. "Why would *we* need to run away?"

"I didn't mean us," I said crossly. Then because he seemed a little crestfallen, I added, "It was just something Jenny brought up."

But I asked him silently: *Oh, Robert, why can't you imagine running away with someone, someone it kills you to be apart from?*

I was thinking once again about things outside our friendship, beyond what we were to each other. Robert could tell—he knew me pretty well by then. It always made him become very quiet. I put my arm around him, not wanting him to be sad. "Never mind," I said. "What do you want to do on Saturday?"

He was still pouting a little. "Well, I guess if you're bored, there are a few stores downtown we could rob."

I laughed. He put his arm around me too and looked down at me, smiling his crooked smile. He was proud of himself whenever he made me laugh. It was one of the things I loved about him. Our foreheads touched. The moment passed.